Thank you

Deadly Diamonds

Ian

Jan '25

Deadly Diamonds

IAN RICHARDSON

THE CHOIR PRESS

First published in the United Kingdom in 2023 by
The Choir Press

ISBN 978-1-78963-342-9

Other books by the author

City Crime
Murder Behind The Screen

Thanks to my wife, Valerie, and children, Holly, Adrian and Ruth for their support.

This novel is inspired by true events that took place in Corsica during the Second World War.

CHAPTER 1
October 1943

Lieutenant Bill Cottrell waited impatiently outside the rundown farmhouse high up in the Corsican mountains. The Germans had recently taken over from the less aggressive Italian troops, and the war was hotting up on this Mediterranean island. Cottrell had been operating undercover here for over a year, and he knew that if he was captured, the Germans would have every legal right to execute him as a spy. He shivered in his overcoat, partly from the night cold and partly from fear.

Cottrell felt the terror every soldier has at the prospect of imminent death. He asked himself what he would miss most. His mind wandered from the warm Mediterranean island where he was now posted, to a typical cold winter's evening in the East End of London near his home. He could almost taste the first pint of bitter with his friends. Later on, he would take his girlfriend, Ethel, for a walk. He smiled in recollection of the late-night kiss that he usually received. Just then, he heard a crack behind him. He instinctively brought his rifle up and pointed it in the direction that the sound came from.

'Don't worry, Lieutenant, it's only me,' came an English voice.

Cottrell relaxed. 'My God, Sergeant, you nearly got yourself killed.'

Tony Gash apologised. 'Sorry, sir,' he said. Gash was a new arrival in Corsica. Cottrell knew him from past training in Aldershot, but he knew Gash had a lot to learn. Just then, he heard the sound he had been expecting. He wordlessly indicated for Gash to hide in the undergrowth.

Within a few seconds, they both saw a German officer walk leisurely out of the farmhouse to his waiting vehicle. Cottrell knew him as Felix Muller, notorious as being the cruellest high-ranking Gestapo member in Corsica. Muller's driver saluted and opened the door for him. The vehicle sped away with Muller smiling in a self-satisfied manner from the back seat. Cottrell waited until the vehicle was out of sight before he and Gash quietly made their way towards the farmhouse.

'Are you sure this is safe, sir?' Gash asked. 'Can we trust this woman?'

'Yes, I'm sure,' Bill Cottrell replied. 'Amelia's on our side. She's helped us in the past.'

'But she's Muller's mistress. How can we be sure she's on our side?'

'I'm sure,' Bill said shortly, as he entered the farmhouse. 'Come with me.'

'Sal"é, Amelia,' Cottrell said, using the Corsican greeting, as he entered the small sitting room. 'This is my new sergeant, Tony Gash.' Despite his sergeant's misgivings, Bill knew Amelia, despite being Muller's mistress, was one of his most useful informants. Gash followed him and nodded respectfully at the attractive young woman, who was tidying the room after her Gestapo visitor had left. Cottrell and Gash were the only people who knew of Amelia's assistance. For greater security, Cottrell never told anyone in the Resistance of her help.

'Bon soir, Bill,' Amelia said, as she tidied up after Muller's visit. 'How are things?'

'Fine. More importantly, have you picked up any information from Muller? Do you know what his next plans are?'

'Yes, Felix is travelling up to Corte to pick up some equipment, then driving down to Bastia.'

'Thank you, Amelia,' Cottrell said. 'I think we will prepare a welcome for him – one that the Germans won't forget.'

'Good luck, Bill,' Amelia said. 'But be careful – and you

2

too,' she said to Gash less warmly, before he followed Cottrell out.

On the edge of the village, Bill was suddenly stopped by a figure dressed in black. Worried he might be a German soldier, Bill tried to hide in the undergrowth.

'Lieutenant Cottrell,' the man called.

Wondering who could know his name, Bill stood up and advanced tentatively. To his partial relief, he recognised a Mafia partisan, with whom he was cooperating. His relief was only partial as he knew that the Mafia could turn on the Allies as easily as they had turned on the Germans. 'My God, is that you, Santoni?'

'Yes, it's me,' Santoni replied. 'You are out late, Lieutenant.'

'Yes, I'm on a mission,' Bill replied. To his relief, Santoni did not press for further information, but merely nodded his understanding and allowed Bill to continue. Bill walked forward while Gash followed a few steps behind.

After a few minutes, Gash suddenly felt someone grab him from behind. The unknown person held his hand over Gash's mouth to stop him from crying out.

'I think you are a British spy,' the man said in a strong German accent. 'If you want to live, don't cry out, or I will kill you.'

The man turned Gash round and removed his hand. Gash immediately recognised him as Muller, the man who had left Amelia's house a few minutes before.

'What is your task, sergeant?' Muller said, as Gash's eyes widened in fear and surprise. 'Yes, you see I know your rank and a lot about you and Lieutenant Cottrell.'

'You know I can't tell you anything,' Gash said.

Muller suddenly took a flick knife from his pocket and held it to Gash's throat. 'I said, what is your task, sergeant?'

Gash quailed at the sight of the flick knife. He knew he should refuse to say anything, but the sharp blade terrified him, and he decided to cooperate. 'We're planning to blow up the bridge a mile up the road while you are crossing over,' he stammered.

'Thank you, Sergeant, now that didn't hurt, did it?'

'No, Herr Muller.'

'I see you know my name, even if you have forgotten my rank. This is what is going to happen. You will not tell your officer about our little chat. If you disobey me, you will die. I have an important task for your officer. If the two of you do what you are told, you will both live. If you reveal anything to your officer, both of you will die. Do you agree to cooperate?'

Gash stared at the flick knife. Too frightened to speak, he merely nodded.

'Good, you are being sensible. Now go,' Muller told the terrified sergeant. He watched as Gash rushed off to join Bill Cottrell.

* * * *

Later that night, Bill Cottrell looked at his watch. It was hard to read in the night-time, but he could make out that it was around 3 am. He looked around at the Corsican landscape as far as he could see it in the moonlight. In normal times, Bill would have enjoyed the smell of eucalyptus, jasmine and rosemary from the maquis – the Corsican undergrowth, which was everywhere on the island – but for now, it was an unwelcome distraction.

From Amelia's information, Cottrell guessed that Felix Muller would be passing over the bridge in front of him very soon. He primed his hand to press the lever to ignite the dynamite just at the time the German convoy would be crossing the bridge. He thought with satisfaction of the damage this would do to the German war effort in this area. He knew of the rumours that the Germans were about to leave Corsica. Everyone expected them to inflict as much damage on the inhabitants as they could while they were still on the island, and, if successful, this raid should distract them.

Bill Cottrell, with his working-class cockney background, could never have imagined being in Corsica in peace time, or indeed being an officer at all. It was only because he happened to speak fluent French that he had been promoted and sent on this dangerous assignment.

The tension on the island of Corsica was almost tangible. The German soldiers were more jittery than they had been up till now. Everyone on the island expected the Americans to invade soon and make the island the first part of France liberated from the Nazis. This made the German troops even more dangerous than usual.

'Are you ready, sir?' Cottrell heard the voice of Tony Gash in his ear.

'Keep an eye out. Tell me when the convoy appears around that bend,' Cottrell told him, keeping his voice quiet, though there did not seem to be anyone nearby.

Cottrell anticipated with satisfaction the thought of Muller's vehicle being blown high into the Corsican sky. This would make a satisfying dent in the Nazi war effort, and make life easier for the local Corsicans, many of whom Cottrell regarded as his friends.

Gash called out 'They're coming,' but before Cottrell could press the explosives charger, he found himself lifted in the air. He was vaguely wondering how the world had turned upside down, when he felt himself being beaten with a rifle butt. He fell unconscious for an unknown period.

When Bill Cottrell awoke, he found himself in the back of a moving vehicle. He tried to move his hands but realised he was handcuffed and was being transported in a German staff car. Looking around, he saw he was being held prisoner by Muller and two of his soldiers. He wondered why his sergeant was not with him but decided, with relief, Gash must have escaped. Cottrell mentally prepared himself for torture and an excruciating death, as he knew the German troops would regard him as a spy without protection of a uniform. The car sped along the mountain road until it arrived at a place Cottrell recognised and dreaded. It was the Gestapo headquarters – high up in the mountains.

Once they had arrived, the Gestapo men dragged Cottrell into the building and down some stone steps. Then they tied him to a chair and threw a bucket of cold water over him. After an hour or so left on his own, Cottrell was expecting the worst. He wondered if Gash had also been captured, but decided it was best to keep silent, in case Gash had escaped without the Germans realising he was there.

When Cottrell's captors pulled the blindfold off him, his worst fears were realised. He was facing Felix Muller. Cottrell knew how much people were terrified of Muller – he was well known as a ruthless man, the worst Gestapo chief of all. Cottrell mentally geared himself up for a short period of torture and then a firing squad. To his amazement, Muller untied Cottrell, gave him a drink of water, then sent the guards out of the room.

'Lieutenant Cottrell, I believe,' Muller said. 'We have been looking for you for a long time. You must have much information to tell me.'

'The only thing I have to say is my name, rank and serial number,' Cottrell muttered in reply.

'That only applies to soldiers in uniform, which you seem to be without. Normally, I would be happy for you to be tortured and shot,' Muller said with a smile devoid of all humour, 'but, at the moment, you may be more useful to me alive.'

Cottrell stared at Muller with suspicion. 'What do you mean?'

'Tell me what you know about when the Allies plan to land in Corsica.'

'I don't know anything about that,' Cottrell said.

Muller looked at Cottrell thoughtfully. 'Somehow I believe you. But I know the Allies will be landing in Corsica soon and I want to hide some valuables. If the Resistance know you are with me, they will be less likely to attack.' Muller stood up. 'This is your lucky day, Lieutenant Cottrell. You are sailing with me to Italy.'

'Italy? What are you talking about? That's a hundred kilometres away.'

Muller ignored Cottrell's further questions as he led him out of the building. He had his gun trained carefully at Cottrell's head. As Muller marched his prisoner to his car, two guards stood to attention. Cottrell gained the impression they were as surprised by this turn of events as he was.

'Sit in the front of the vehicle, Lieutenant,' Muller said. 'I want the partisans to see you, so they won't shoot up the car.'

'Where are we going?' Cottrell asked.

'Bastia harbour. I have commandeered a fine yacht there. First I will blindfold you.'

After around an hour, the vehicle came to a stop. Muller pulled the blindfold from Bill's eyes. Bill blinked in the bright sunshine then gazed at the scene in Bastia harbour. He had been here many times before, but the scene looked very different now. At first sight the sky was oddly beautiful, with bright red flares streaming across it. For a moment, it reminded him of firework parties in his youth. People were running round in the darkness as Cottrell imagined they used to in the days before the war. There was a strong smell of gunpowder, which again reminded him of fireworks.

In a moment, he realised that the scene was of the Germans about to evacuate Corsica. The bright lights in the sky were from explosions caused by aerial bombardment from the United States Air Force. What at first sight seemed like celebratory fireworks were in fact artillery and the screams were not of joy but of death. Muller stabbed a gun into Bill's back. 'Keep moving, we're escaping by sea.'

Bill turned his eyes from the sky above to the yacht moored near him. His mind had only just taken in the surroundings when Muller stabbed him again with his gun. 'Get moving. With any luck when they see your uniform the Americans won't try to sink this boat.'

It was obvious that the rumour that the Allies were about to land in Corsica had spread, and the German troops were making preparations to leave before they could be captured by the Allies. Several senior German officers could be seen boarding various types of craft. Muller had driven his car next to a particularly luxurious yacht. 'This is the vessel we will be sailing in,' Muller said. 'I bought it for a very reasonable price.'

'You mean you stole it,' Cottrell said.

'If you like,' Muller replied, with a thin smile. 'Now help me load these safe deposit boxes.'

Cottrell hesitated, until Muller hit him in the back with his revolver. Cottrell fell to the ground, then, realising the hopelessness of his position, climbed to his feet, and carried the safe deposit boxes from the staff car onto the yacht. Muller took care to keep his gun trained on Cottrell at all times. Once the suitcase and boxes were loaded, Muller ordered Cottrell onto the yacht and ordered him to cast off.

Cottrell obeyed Muller's orders. He could see the Gestapo man was shaking with nerves, which would probably make him even more dangerous than usual. After a few minutes, with Cottrell at the helm and Muller beside him, the yacht cleared the entrance to Bastia harbour. The journey continued out to sea and Bill manoeuvred the yacht out of sight of the harbour. Then, after around half an hour's sailing, the yacht suddenly crashed onto rocks, with a frightening shudder. The large boom collapsed, making a deafening noise, and Bill saw Muller fall unconscious under its weight.

Bill was unsure what to do next. At first, he gave a silent cheer that his captor was either dead or unconscious, and he would no longer have to obey Muller's barked orders. However, very soon, it occurred to him that his position as the sole person on the large yacht was if anything worse than before.

After a few minutes trying to remove water from the yacht while watching it sink even further, Cottrell decided his position was hopeless. He was unsure of his exact location, but he knew he could not be far from the shore. Looking at the deck, he saw that one of the safe deposit boxes had broken open and, instinctively, he grabbed three bags that he guessed contained diamonds or other valuables. Bill jumped into the sea, and started to swim, holding the bags in one hand. He saw no sign of Muller as he swam and assumed the Gestapo chief must have drowned.

After some time, Cottrell finally reached the shore and dragged himself onto some rocks. He rested a few minutes to get his breath back, before deciding what to do next. Turning around, he saw some farm buildings a few hundred yards away, which he felt should provide limited shelter and protection from any stray bombardment. Bill wondered whether to make himself known to whoever was living in the farmhouse, but after a moment's reflection told himself that some Corsicans were in the pay of the Germans and might pass him over to the local Gestapo. Even if the farmer and his family supported the Resistance, there seemed no reason to expose them to danger by asking them for help. Bill walked cautiously into the barn, hoping there was no one else there.

Once inside, Cottrell could not hear or see anyone else, and decided to hide on the top floor of the barn. Covering himself with straw, he tried to warm himself up. After a while, he stopped shivering, and started to take stock of his predicament, trying to make sense of what had just happened to him. How had Muller managed to capture him? For a long time, he lay there wondering if someone had betrayed him to the Germans. All the evidence pointed to Amelia. Bill instinctively felt she was on his side, but she may have had no choice but to betray him if Muller had tortured her if he learnt about her help for the Resistance. Santoni also knew about Bill's whereabouts, but he found it hard to believe the Mafia man would betray his own country. Bill had no reason to be suspicious of Tony Gash, and was only pleased that, somehow, his sergeant had managed to escape. Eventually, Bill Cottrell fell asleep, to the grunts of wild boar rooting around for food outside the barn.

CHAPTER 2

Later that day, from her farmhouse near Corte, Amelia saw American aircraft flying low over the island. Once they were overhead, parachutists jumped from the planes and floated down. She realised the long-awaited liberation of the island of Corsica had started. She was pleased that one curse – the hated presence of the Nazis in general, and Felix Muller, in particular – was almost over. However, she guessed that another curse for her – that of the revenge of the partisans – was about to start. She locked and barricaded her front door, but, hiding behind an upturned table, she knew it would do no good against a determined mob.

That night, Amelia heard the sound of a crowd outside her front door. They called for her to come out, but knowing what was in store, she hid behind her table. At around midnight, she saw the door gradually being forced open by a large crowd of her angry neighbours. Within about five minutes, the door broke down and a swarthy man she recognised as a leading member of the local Resistance stood before her. She knew he was Santoni, and he was the head of the local Mafia family.

'Come out and face justice, Amelia Luri, you whore,' he called.

Amelia nervously emerged from her hiding place.

'Wait, you do not understand,' she called. 'I helped the Resistance ...' But the mob took no notice. They shaved her head and started to strip her. Amelia fainted as the mob cheered her humiliation.

* * * *

After sunrise on the following day, Bill Cottrell woke up in his uncomfortable hiding place in the barn. He stretched and started to remove the straw on which he had been sleeping from his clothes and wondered what had woken him. Then he heard a jeep driving up to the farmhouse. He tried to listen to what the troops were saying, and eventually recognised the welcome sound of English, spoken by an American GI. Cottrell crawled down the rickety steps of the barn and walked cautiously out of hiding with his arms raised high. He carefully approached the platoon leader.

'Why, what do we have here?' the platoon leader sneered, in a Brooklyn accent.

'I am Lieutenant William Cottrell, of the British Army, working undercover,' he said.

The platoon leader stared at him, suspiciously. 'We'll have to see about that. We've had plenty of Germans pretending to be on our side, many sounding just as English as you do. We spotted them pretty damned quickly. If you're a German, admit it now and save everyone's time.'

'No. I'm what I say I am. Check with your headquarters.'

The platoon leader merely grunted, though it seemed that something about Bill's story seemed believable to him. 'Sit down with your hands on your head, and keep your mouth shut,' he growled.

After an hour, Cottrell was taken under armed guard in a jeep to the newly-established US Army mobile headquarters outside Bastia. Bill could hear a few phone calls being made. Gradually, the guards seemed to become more friendly, until, after an hour, his identity was confirmed. He was released and allowed to join the GIs in the army canteen, enjoying his first meal of American-style food.

A few days later, Cottrell flew back to England on an American plane. On the flight back, he opened the bags he had taken from the yacht for the first time and stared with shock at several large diamonds. Bill ran the diamonds through his fingers. They glistened in the artificial light of the plane. Unsure of what to do, he put them back into his pocket. He was worried that he may have been noticed, but he looked round and, as far as he could tell, no one had seen him.

He thought of Muller's body lying in the yacht and was confident the cruel Gestapo chief had died. No one else alive knew he was in possession of the diamonds and Cottrell decided to keep them safe in his keeping. He did not know that Muller, far from being dead, had managed to escape from the wrecked yacht. He had swum to shore and found a place on one of the last German troopships to leave Corsica.

Chapter 3
1945

After returning to Germany in 1943, Muller had been assigned to the disastrous German invasion of Russia. By early 1945, in the last days of the war, Felix Muller found himself among a large group of German soldiers who were surrendering to the Russian invading force. One Russian soldier pointed his rifle at Muller and uttered an order in his own language, which Muller could not understand. Muller put up his hands in the universal symbol of surrender. He could tell the Russian soldier was wondering if it was a trick and Muller feared he would be killed. He was relieved when the soldier merely indicated for him to join a queue of prisoners of war making their way to the nearest camp.

Muller realised with relief that his war was at an end. As he queued up for a bowl of thin soup and some stale bread, another German officer behind him tried to make conversation. 'This is terrible,' the stranger said. 'It is the end of Germany. The end of civilisation. These Russian barbarians have won. What is going to happen to our country?'

Muller shrugged. He was indifferent to the fate of the Third Reich and held all governments in contempt. All he knew was that, for the most part, and certainly while in Corsica, he had enjoyed the war. He was a small-time criminal before it began and became a bigger one once he had put on his uniform. The Gestapo had given him free rein to steal whatever he could – both for the Third Reich and also for himself.

He thought, with regret, of those safe deposit boxes in the bottom of the sea near Bastia, but then shrugged his shoulders. Such setbacks were part of a criminal's career. He proposed to continue being a career criminal in whatever future might lie before him. He imagined it would not be long before he was released from a prisoner of war camp, and with Germany in ruins, he visualised a profitable career in smuggling goods to make money from the poor.

CHAPTER 4

A few months after VE day, Bill Cottrell looked at his reflection in the Woolworths shop window near his home, close to the bombed-out London docks. After five years in uniform, it seemed strange to be wearing this brown demob suit. He had spent an exciting couple of years after leaving Corsica taking part in the Liberation of France. He had enjoyed being cheered by the crowds welcoming the Allied soldiers as they entered each village and town along the way.

Bill told himself, with a sigh of regret, that he now had to decide how to make his way in life as a civilian. With so many soldiers returning from the war, he knew how difficult it was to find a job. Overall, he had enjoyed his time in the army. It gave his life a structure it had lacked before, and he knew that three square meals and a steady income had made his situation more comfortable in the army than it was as the unemployed civilian he had now become. He looked at the goods for sale in the shop window and wondered how he could afford them with no job.

'What are you doing there, son? You look up to no good.' Cottrell jumped at the authoritative voice behind him. He turned around and saw a large police constable looking down at him with a scowl.

'Oh, nothing, officer. I was just on my way home.'

'Well, make sure you go there, then. I don't want to see you hanging round here again. Good night to you.'

'Good night, officer.' Cottrell obediently turned back to walk to his digs, then stopped to watch the constable carry on his beat. It occurred to him that there were many similarities between the army and the police. He told himself he could make a successful

15

career as a police officer. He felt it should provide a reasonable income, and he knew that with his good record in the army, they would be likely to accept him. Having made this decision, he felt cheerful about his prospects for the first time since the war had ended.

Before applying to join the police, he had the issue of what to do with the diamonds he had kept from that trove in Corsica. He supposed they must have belonged to someone, but obviously not to Muller, the Nazi thug who had forced him to transport them. Money from their sale would be a very useful start to his career. There was something ironic in starting off a police career with a dishonest act, but he told himself these were strange times.

A few days later, Bill Cottrell entered a working-class pub, close to his home. He went over to the public bar, where he was due to meet his wartime colleague, Tony Gash. He ordered a pint, when he heard a familiar voice behind him.

'Hello, Lieutenant,' Gash said. 'How are things?'

'Hello, Sergeant,' Cottrell said, taking in Gash's civilian suit, which was smarter than his own. 'But the army days are behind us now, aren't they? We're civilians now.'

'Very well, Bill,' Gash said. 'If you're buying, I'll have a pint of the Best.'

Cottrell bought two pints and the two men retreated to a table away from the hubbub of people around them.

'It's good to meet up again, Tony,' Bill said. 'We haven't spoken since that night I was captured, have we?'

'Yes, I was sorry I couldn't help you, but there were too many of them. I knew there was no point in both of us getting caught by the Germans. I guess Muller's mistress gave us away. At least I could pass the news to London by radio, so they knew what was going on.'

'Yes, you're probably right. Muller seemed to know his days in Corsica were numbered, and he wasn't too hard on me,' Bill said, sipping his beer.

'Whatever happened to Muller? Is he still alive?'

'No, I'm sure he's dead.' Bill felt guilty about the diamonds he had retained and decided it was safest not to tell Gash about the ill-fated yacht voyage that Muller had forced him to take.

'So, have you decided what to do now you're on civvy street?' Gash asked, after a pause.

'I'm not sure, but I met a policeman the other day,' Cottrell said. 'It got me thinking. I've decided I might do quite well as a copper.'

'That could be a good career for you, telling people what to do,' Gash said. 'You were always bossy enough when we were in the army,' he added, with a smile.

'And how about you, Tony?' Cottrell asked.

'Oh, I'll go back and join the family business – my dad is a jeweller, and he says he'll take me on and teach me the trade,' Gash said. 'If I do well, I could take over from him when the time comes.'

'That sounds a promising career for you, Tony,' Cottrell said. After a few sips of beer, he delicately broached a subject that was on his mind. 'Tell me, Tony, your family's in the business. Where would someone go if they had diamonds to sell?'

Gash looked up in surprise. 'Why do you want to know?' Cottrell shrugged. 'The main traders are all in Hatton Garden,' Gash said, after a pause.

'Where's that?'

'In the City of London,' Gash replied.

Cottrell felt the bag of diamonds in his pocket and decided to visit Hatton Garden to sell the diamonds the next day before he applied to join the police. He had no wish to share his earnings with Gash, and swiftly moved the conversation to the neutral subject of football. Bill was relieved that Gash seemed to have soon forgotten his uncharacteristic question.

* * * *

Two days later, Bill walked out of a diamond traders' establishment in Hatton Garden. He no longer had the diamonds, but he had the unimaginable sum of five hundred pounds in his pocket. He had been to several dealers, many of whom had looked at him suspiciously and refused to deal with him. Eventually, he had found one prepared to buy the diamonds without asking too many questions.

Bill told himself that, no doubt, he had sold the diamonds too cheaply, but he had enough to buy a house outright. He should be able to marry Ethel, the girlfriend he had left behind when he went to war, and perhaps start a family. He told himself that while the diamonds may have been stolen originally, he felt he was perhaps putting them to a good cause. A few weeks later, Bill Cottrell had joined the police force and become engaged. He felt he should have a successful career in front of him.

Chapter 5
1989

In late 1989, Felix Muller was sitting in a bar in East Berlin, sipping a cognac. Muller had acquired a taste for cognac while in Corsica and still drank it occasionally as a special treat. By and large, he was feeling pleased with life in general, as the expensive alcohol slipped down his throat.

Muller reflected that, for the past four decades, he had done very well out of the post-war division of Germany. The East German regime thought the Berlin Wall near him was impregnable, but he knew otherwise. Running a black-market in luxuries from West to East Germany had given Muller a healthy income. This day, he had arranged a delivery of consumer goods from the West and was awaiting their arrival. He had enough experience to know what steps to take to ensure the East German border guards did not stop his lucrative trade.

Glancing across the table, Muller looked in a self-satisfied way at the nineteen-year-old blonde bar hostess seated opposite him. Muller appreciated the way that Zoe always attracted attention when they were out together. He did not care that they looked an unlikely couple. He would often overhear people say that Zoe was only with him because of his money. Muller knew they were right and saw no reason to be ashamed of the fact. He reached out and stroked her hair, symbolising his control over her. Zoe smiled dutifully back. She knew that the only hope for advancement, for a young girl in the seedy world she had been brought up in, was to be supported by a man with money, however old and unattractive he might be.

Suddenly, on the television in the bar, Muller saw pictures of the crowds streaming through the Berlin Wall. This would have been inconceivable even one week before. Muller regarded the people driving through the border in their Trabant cars with contempt.

'They don't realise how pathetic they look to people in the West,' he said. 'Look at their cars – they're years behind.'

'What do you think will happen to us in East Berlin now, Felix?' Zoe asked.

'I've no idea. This is terrible news. My business is flogging goods from one part of Germany to another. If the wall collapses, my whole income disappears.'

'Don't worry. I'm sure you'll find some other way of making money,' Zoe said.

Muller was about to swear at Zoe for making such an apparently stupid remark, but then realised she was probably right. It was obvious to Muller that the fall of East Germany was imminent, but there was no time to regret this. He knew that his type of criminality would be profitable in whatever system of government operated in Germany.

Muller wondered what his next career move might be. He knew he was growing old for a criminal career and had no doubt that younger men were looking for ways to take over his smuggling activities. He hoped for some large heist to enable him to live the rest of his life in comfort. One advantage of the likely new regime was that East Germans would now be able to travel abroad as they wished. He had done well under the Nazis and being a Gestapo chief in Corsica had been the high point of his criminal career. He told himself that the capitalist united Germany that was likely to be created soon would similarly offer a man of his criminal abilities scope for advancement.

Muller knew he just had to find the right way to maximise his illegal income. He thought back to those hectic days before he was forced out of Corsica by the Allies. He decided he would operate in Berlin for a few years and build up the resources needed to recover the treasure that he had once possessed. He knew that it lay hidden somewhere off the coast of Corsica, where his yacht had sunk.

'You might be right, Zoe,' Muller said, in uncharacteristic good humour. 'Somewhere in the Mediterranean, there is a whole lot of money just waiting for me.'

Zoe could not imagine what he meant by that remark but decided not to ask further questions. She had experienced several painful injuries at Muller's hands when he was angry, which she accepted as part of the lifestyle she had adopted. She finished her drink, pleased that Muller was, for once, in a good mood.

CHAPTER 6
1994

Detective Sergeant Philippa Cottrell of the City of London police stretched out on the beach at her hotel near Bastia. She felt the new bikini she had bought for this holiday showed her figure off rather well. Looking out across the white sands, she saw a couple of good-looking young Corsican men prowling the beach for young women. As a twenty-six-year-old single woman, she told herself she would quite enjoy being chatted up by one of them, just for the pleasure of turning them down. She was used to attracting men, who largely disappeared when she displayed her police warrant card. Then Philippa remembered the reason she had come to Corsica in the first place. She smiled with affection as she looked across to her grandfather sitting on a towel next to her. She had always respected Bill Cottrell both as a man and a former police officer, and he had played a large part in encouraging her to choose a police career. Philippa's parents had been killed in a car crash when Philippa was still young, and Bill had been more like a father than a grandfather to her.

Recently, her grandfather had told her for the first time that he had served in Corsica during the war and wanted to return for a sightseeing visit. His health was declining, and he was about to move to a retirement home. Philippa had no ties at present and welcomed his company on a Corsican holiday. She reflected that he looked comically out of place among the lovely young things on the beach – rather like the cliché picture of an elderly British tourist.

A waitress came up to Bill. She instinctively guessed he was

British and addressed him in English. 'Would you like a drink, sir?' she asked. 'We can get you English tea, if you like.'

'Non, merci, je voudrais un citron presse,' Bill replied in perfect French.

The waitress tried in vain to hide her shock at his fluency in her native language. 'Bien sur, monsieur. Mille pardons,' she said as she walked away to fulfil his order.

'Why should that girl be surprised I speak French? I was speaking it before she was born,' Bill muttered grumpily.

'I don't know, Grandad. Somehow you do look English though,' Philippa said, with a slight smile. 'You are enjoying the holiday, aren't you?' she asked, trying to cheer him up.

Bill looked around at the beach and the high-rise hotels. 'Oh, yes, down here on the coast it's lovely, but it's not how it was during the war,' he said, pointing toward the south. 'I was up in the mountains then.'

'Everything is bound to feel different now,' Philippa said. 'You were a young man in those days, and you were fighting the Germans. We're on holiday in peacetime now. Corsica's bound to have changed.'

'Yes, yes, I know, but I would like to see some of the old places I remember, Philippa love. Please can you take me up there?'

'Are you sure you want to go, Grandad? Why not just enjoy your holiday? Look at everyone having fun on the beach. Sometimes it's not good to go back.'

Bill nodded. 'I'm sure. I've been thinking about this for fifty years, and I want to go to the mountains to see how things have changed.'

Philippa glanced at her grandfather and realised his mind was made up. 'Very well, Grandad. If you really want to go, I'll hire a car tomorrow,' she said, picking up her mobile phone to make the arrangements.

* * * *

23

The next day, once inside their hire car, Philippa turned to Bill. 'Well, Grandad, where shall we go?' she asked.

'I'd like to relive that final couple of days when the Germans left. It all started at Amelia's house near Corte. Can we go there?'

'Who's Amelia?' Philippa asked, with a smile. 'Someone I should know about?'

'She was the girlfriend of Muller. He was the Gestapo thug who arrested me. Amelia used to give us information on where Muller would be. She was very useful to us. I've always thought she was the person who betrayed me to Muller. She must have been tortured by the Gestapo to betray me, and I wanted to tell her I forgive her.'

Philippa looked across at her grandfather dubiously. 'Are you sure about making this trip, Grandad?' She asked. 'Sometimes it's best to leave the past behind.'

'I'm sure. I can't rest until I find out what really happened.'

Philippa sighed. 'Very well, I could drive you there, but there's no guarantee that this woman still lives in the same house – even if she's still alive. Don't forget it was over fifty years ago when you last saw her.'

'I know all that, but can you take me there anyway?' Bill asked.

Philippa realised her grandfather was determined to make this trip. 'I'll take you to Corte, Grandad, but don't be surprised if things have changed.'

* * * *

Two hours later, Bill and Philippa were parked outside a stone-built house in the Corsican mountains. 'Is this the place?' Philippa asked.

'Yes, this is it. It looks just the same,' Bill said, opening the window. 'Can you smell the maquis?'

'The what?'

'The local undergrowth has this amazing smell of eucalyptus, juniper and all sorts of other plants. This reminds me of that last evening before I was captured by the Germans. The local resistance was called the Maquis, as well. They were tough, believe me. Even the Gestapo were scared of them.'

'That's interesting, Grandad, but what do you want to do now?' Philippa said, looking round nervously. The grey house nestled by the equally grey mountains had filled her with a sense of dread.

'We could walk up and knock on Amelia's door,' Bill suggested.

'I really don't think that's a good idea, Grandad,' Philippa said. 'Even if she's alive, she'll be an old woman now and may be married with a family. She probably wants to forget the war. She won't want any old soldiers reappearing. You say she may have betrayed you. What if she was really a German sympathiser all along?'

Bill thought for a moment. 'You may be right, Philippa love,' he said, 'but can I just walk around here for old times' sake?'

Philippa nodded agreement, as she switched off the car's ignition. Bill opened the car door, then started to walk along the road. Just then the front door of the house opened, and an elderly lady appeared in typical black Corsican dress. She walked down the steps of the house, when she suddenly stopped. It was obvious to Philippa, watching from the car, that the woman had seen Bill and recognised him. Philippa could see them talking but kept out of sight.

'William?' the woman said, turning. 'It can't be you, after all these years. But it is, isn't it?' The woman seemed to be about to faint.

'Yes, it's me, Amelia,' Bill said, putting out his arm, to stop Amelia from falling. 'I'm sorry to give you such a shock. My granddaughter and I are on holiday in Bastia, and I wanted to come to see you. I often think about the war years.'

'To be honest, I try to forget about those days,' she said, looking round to make sure they were not being overheard. 'It's great you came to see me, but don't stay too long, will you? I don't want anyone to see you.'

'But how have you been all these years?' he asked.

'Life was hell for me after the Liberation,' Amelia said, with a shiver. 'You don't want to know the things the Resistance people did to me. Parading me through the streets with my head shaved was the least of it. They said I was a traitor and a whore. That was a long time ago, of course, and things are quieter now, but a lot of my neighbours still won't talk to me.'

'I'm so sorry about that. I know you helped the Resistance when you could – right until the end,' Bill said, then paused, as he raised a difficult subject. 'Amelia, I suppose I should hate you for giving me away that day, but I know they were difficult times. I wanted to say I forgive you. I'm guessing Muller forced you to tell him what you knew.'

'What do you mean?' Amelia asked, staring at Bill. 'I didn't give you away. I was as shocked as anyone when I heard the Gestapo had captured you.'

'But someone must have betrayed me. Muller seemed to know about everything. He captured me as soon as I got to that bridge.'

Amelia gave a half-smile. 'Think about it. Who else knew about your mission?'

'No one, apart from you, and Tony Gash, of course,' Bill paused, then caught Amelia's expression. 'You don't mean Gash, do you? He was a friend. He couldn't be a traitor.'

'Think what you like, William,' Amelia said. 'All I can tell you is it wasn't me.'

'But Tony was with me all the time. He couldn't have given me away,' Bill paused. 'Though in the darkness, I couldn't see where he was all the time. I've often wondered how he escaped when Muller caught me. Tony always said he just got lucky and Muller didn't see him. Unless …'

Amelia interrupted. 'I think I've told you all I know. Now go, before the neighbours start asking questions.'

'I saw Santoni that night. Was he one of the people who lynched you?'

'He was the worst of them. When I think of all the criminal things he has done… How could he claim to be better than me?'

'I kept your help secret, Amelia. I thought it was best. I'm sorry I wasn't there to protect you.'

'It was your job to get back to England and continue fighting,' Amelia said, and touched Bill's arm. 'Now I must go.'

Bill stared after Amelia as she walked away, then he returned to Philippa, who was waiting in the car.

'Can we move on, Philippa?' he said. 'You're right, coming here was a mistake.'

Philippa switched on the ignition of the car. 'Are you sure you don't want to stay longer? You look upset. Wasn't she pleased to see you?'

'No, you're right. I shouldn't have come back,' Bill said. 'I don't need to see Amelia again. It's enough to know that she's still alive.'

'So, what did you talk about?'

'I wanted to say I forgave her for betraying me to Muller, but she said it wasn't her.'

'So, who was the traitor?'

Bill looked at Philippa with tears in his eyes. 'She said it was my sergeant. I thought he was a friend of mine. He couldn't have done it, could he? I think I'd kill him if I thought it was him.'

Philippa hugged her grandfather. 'Come along, Granddad, you've got to put those days behind you. You can't keep worrying about what happened fifty years ago. Let's get you down to the beach so we can enjoy the rest of the holiday.'

Bill looked straight ahead. 'The past is all I have to think about now,' he said to himself.

As Philippa prepared to drive the two of them away, a top-of-the range black Mercedes rushed past and nearly sideswiped her car. A dangerous-looking elderly man was reading a paper in the back seat, and he seemed not to notice her. Philippa swore to herself as she brought the car to a stop. She saw that her grandfather had ducked down when he saw the man in the car.

'Who the hell was that?' Philippa asked. 'And why does he have to drive like a maniac?'

'I recognise that man from the war. He's Santoni – one of the Mafia leaders,' Bill said. 'They think they own this part of Corsica – and they do. We always had to be careful we didn't tread on their toes during our operations. I thought he must have been dead now, but I can see he and his family still control the area. You don't want to tangle with them. I'm glad he didn't see me.'

'This seems like a dangerous place,' Philippa said. She tried to sound light-hearted, but as she looked round at the mountainous roads and occasional political graffiti written in the local Corsican language, she felt vaguely threatened. She had a strong desire to take her grandfather somewhere less dangerous. 'So, shall we leave the mountains and drive back down to the coast? It should be safer there.'

'Yes, please, Philippa love, let's go back to the coast. There are too many painful memories up here.'

* * * *

Two hours later, Philippa had driven down to a headland close to the port of Bastia. They were looking out over the peaceful Mediterranean Sea. 'This seems much more pleasant, Grandad. The sea looks lovely and blue,' she said.

Bill grunted. 'It looks fine now. You don't want to be out in it in the middle of the night in a thundering storm. This is where the yacht that Muller made me crew him on capsized and sank. At least Muller must have drowned, which was one good thing. He was a cruel and horrible man. They called him the Beast of Bastia,' Bill said with a shudder. 'I had to hide in that shed over there,' he said, pointing at a derelict farm building. 'The Americans landed soon afterwards, and I got a free flight back to London.'

'It all sounds exciting,' Philippa said, trying to bring her grandfather's thoughts back to the present day. 'It's hard to believe there was a war here. It seems so peaceful now.'

Bill nodded. He suddenly looked like the old man he was, and it was obvious he no longer wished to talk. 'It was a long time ago. Things are different now. Let's go back to the hotel, Philippa love,' he said, falling asleep immediately.

CHAPTER 7

That evening, Bill stayed in his room, while Philippa went downstairs. She looked around at the crowded restaurant of their hotel, wondering where to find a seat. Philippa walked over to take the only few spaces left in the restaurant. The only other occupant of the table was a good-looking youngish man finishing his meal. He introduced himself as Karl.

'How do you do?' Karl said. 'I'm from Rotterdam. Are you enjoying your holiday?'

'Oh, yes,' Philippa said, who welcomed the chance to talk to a young man nearer her own age, after a day of hearing war reminiscences from her grandfather. 'My grandfather and I went up to Corte – up in the mountains, today. Then we drove up to the headland not far from Bastia. It's incredibly remote there – it's like another world. My grandfather was here in Corsica during the war.'

'Oh, yes, do you know that people are still looking for treasure from the war? Look at that huge gin palace in the bay,' Karl said, pointing to a yacht on the horizon that Philippa estimated would cost at least a million pounds. 'That belongs to a rich American called Link – Edwin Link. He has some crazy idea to find gold in the area. He comes back every year to look for treasure.'

'Oh, yes, and has he found any yet?'

'Not as far as anyone knows.'

Philippa was about to ask more about the yacht but decided to change the subject. 'And what's your job, Karl?'

'Oh, I work for the Dutch government here in Corsica. It's a fascinating island.' Karl turned to Philippa. 'If you like, I could show you some of the sights tomorrow.'

Philippa half smiled at Karl's obvious pick-up line. 'That might be nice,' she replied. 'My grandfather's with me on holiday, but he can manage on his own for a day.'

* * * *

The next morning, Philippa waited in the foyer of the hotel. She had not gone out with an eligible man for over a year and was feeling like an excited schoolgirl. She smiled as she saw Karl arriving at the agreed time.

'I'm glad you could make it,' she said, gently touching his arm.

'I'm looking forward to showing you some of the island, Philippa. My car's at your disposal. What would you like to see?'

'I'm in your hands. I don't know much about Corsica.'

Karl thought for a while. 'How about a trip on the Corsican railway? It's much more interesting than driving.'

Philippa stared at Karl. 'I didn't know they had a railway here.'

'Indeed they do. You know the fast modern trains they have in mainland France – very sleek and modern?'

'Yes, of course.'

'Well, this is the opposite,' Karl said, with a smile. 'It is small, slow and old.'

'I'm intrigued. I'm in your hands.'

A few minutes later, Karl was leading Philippa onto an ancient carriage on the narrow-gauge railway at Bastia station.

'How old is this thing?' Philippa asked.

'It was built in the nineteenth century. It hasn't changed much since and some of the carriages are very old as you can see, but it makes a nice trip. We'll travel up to Calvi – have you heard of it?'

'No, I don't think so.'

'It is an old castle surrounded by a city. Your Lord Nelson lost his eye there.'

'Oh, I didn't know that.'

'We have to change at Ponte Leccia.'

The light tourist talk from Karl continued as the train travelled

31

up the northern coast of Corsica to Calvi, which proved as picturesque as he had described it. Karl showed Philippa some of the sights of the walled city.

'So, what made you visit Corsica?' Karl asked, as they walked along.

'Well, as I told you, my Granddad was here during the war. He wanted to visit here before he got too old. I am enjoying it, I must say.'

'And what's your job?'

'Oh, I'm a detective sergeant in the City of London police,' Philippa replied, then laughed at Karl's surprised expression. 'Don't worry. No one I meet believes I am a police officer, but I love it.'

'I didn't tell you want my job is. I'm in Interpol – only a civilian, I'm afraid, but I'm the liaison point with the Corsican police, so I know them quite well.'

'It sounds as if we have a lot in common,' Philippa said.

The day passed in a pleasant fashion until they took the railway back to Bastia. Philippa felt she would be happy to spend more time with Karl. They seemed to be able to chat freely – both about the highs and lows of police work, and life as a young single in the 1990s. They found they shared similar views on current films and music. Overall, Philippa felt sad that she was due to return home the next day. Karl took Philippa back to her hotel.

'I've had a lovely day, thank you, Karl,' Philippa said and pecked Karl on his cheek. 'It's a pity I have to return to London tomorrow.'

'I'm sad, too. Well, goodbye, Philippa. I've enjoyed our day together,' said Karl as he left after giving her a gentle hug.

Philippa looked after Karl. She felt slightly disappointed that she was unlikely to see him again, but then cast him from her mind, as she returned to her room to see how her grandfather was. Bill seemed to have had an enjoyable day, apparently amazing the hotel staff again with his fluent French. Philippa was pleased he seemed to have forgotten about his upsetting visit to Amelia.

The next day, Bill and Philippa flew back to London. Philippa was pleased that her grandfather had satisfied his wish to return to his old haunts, before he was due to go into a retirement home in a month's time. She prepared to return to her police duties, never expecting to visit Corsica again.

CHAPTER 8

A week later, Tony Gash walked down the corridor of his Beckenham home, to answer the insistent ring on the doorbell. He opened the front door with some annoyance. At seventy-three years of age, he still worked part-time at his family business. He had a few aches and pains associated with his age, but, overall, he was feeling that his life in semi-retirement was good. He was used to quiet in the evening to watch his favourite television programmes and did not welcome visitors.

Once he had opened the front door, he stared in surprise. His old army colleague, Bill Cottrell, stood there. 'Bill, what are you doing here?' Gash asked after a stunned pause.

'Hello, Tony. May I come in?' Bill said, unsmiling, and entered the house without waiting for an answer.

'What's this all about, Bill?' Gash asked, as his visitor entered his living room. Gash was shocked by Bill's visit and by his unfriendly demeanour.

'I've been back to Corsica, Tony. It was my first visit since the war.'

'Oh, really, that must have brought back memories,' Gash replied vaguely, obviously wondering where this discussion was heading. 'In some ways those were great days. We were young then.'

'Not everything was great then, was it though, Tony? I went up to Amelia's old cottage – you remember where we saw Muller leave that last day before I was captured,' Bill said, keeping his eyes fixed on Gash's face.

'I remember,' Gash replied quietly.

'I spoke to Amelia – she still lives in the same house.'

34

'Amelia – Muller's mistress,' Gash said slowly. 'I never trusted her.'

'Yes, she was Muller's mistress,' Bill said, 'and one of the bravest women I've ever known. I wanted to tell her I forgave her for betraying me that day. I said I realised Muller must have tortured her in some way to make her talk. Do you know what she said?'

'Go ahead, Bill,' Gash replied without emotion.

'She said she never told Muller about me. Do you know who she thought must have betrayed me?'

'I have no idea,' Gash replied, shifting uneasily in his chair.

'She said it was you. I've always wondered how you managed to escape, Tony. It would explain everything if you had betrayed me to the Nazis, and they let you leave.'

Gash drew a deep breath. 'I didn't betray you, Bill. I saw you captured by around four Germans. I realised I couldn't do anything if I tried to intervene. I decided it was my duty to escape when I could. I would have been no use to the army if I had tried to rescue you. I would have ended up a prisoner myself. The Allies would have lost two men instead of just you. I'm sorry you were caught, but I didn't betray you.'

'I don't believe you, Tony,' Bill said. He looked around at the military memorabilia on Gash's walls. 'I see you're still involved in the British Legion. What would your friends there say if they knew you were a traitor?'

'I've told you I didn't betray you, Bill. If you'd rather believe a Nazi man's mistress over one of your colleagues, I can't stop you. If you've nothing else to say, I think you'd better leave.'

'Oh, I'll leave all right,' Bill said, standing up. 'Like you, I'm getting older.' He took out a small card. 'I'm moving to a retirement home soon. If you want to get anything off your chest, just call me. Perhaps you'll feel it will ease your conscience – if you have one – to confess. If you want to talk, I'll be at this address.'

Bill stood up and walked out of Gash's house. Gash was too stunned to accompany his visitor to the door but sat in shock as he heard Bill slam it behind him.

CHAPTER 9

A month after Bill and Philippa's visit to Corsica, Felix Muller blinked at the bright sun outside the terminal at Bastia airport as he prepared to go through passport control. He was terrified that he might be recognised. He knew that any Corsican who had survived the war would remember the name of the Beast of Bastia and chose the desk with a young-looking Customs official. He was relieved his name seemed to mean nothing to the young officer manning the desk that he had chosen.

While waiting in the queue, looking at the distant mountains, Muller cast his mind back over the fifty years since he had last been in Corsica. He had enjoyed his time on the island, especially sensing the fear of civilians as they saw him pass by in his chauffeured vehicle. Since the collapse of East Germany five years before, Muller, as he had anticipated, had amassed a useful sum of money from new criminal activities. He felt the time was now right to try to get hold of Rommel's treasure that he had been forced to leave behind at the bottom of the sea when the Nazis left Corsica.

As he walked out of the terminal, Muller felt the welcome sensation of the hot sun warming up his seventy-five-year-old body. He reflected that this was the first time he had been able to visit the site of his wartime experiences. Muller had a good idea of how much the older generation of Corsicans hated him. Every time someone of about his own age passed him, Muller instinctively pulled his sun hat down to avoid being recognised.

Muller had few ties in Berlin and not many people would realise he was missing from his old haunts. The one exception was Zoe, who would be shocked that he had disappeared. He had left a note and some money on their kitchen table. Despite their huge age difference, Muller had something close to affection for her, and felt slightly guilty leaving her behind without saying goodbye. He salved any feelings of guilt by telling himself the money he had placed on the kitchen table should enable her to settle up any debts he had left behind. Muller had spent his life without forming any ties and he felt perhaps it was good to leave before Zoe and he became too entangled. He resolved to put Zoe behind him, telling himself that she would soon find some rich man to support her.

Looking around, Muller told himself that Corsica seemed very different to how it had been that dramatic day in 1943 when the German troops were forced off the island by the Americans. The scent of the maquis still wafted across the island, and he could hear the occasional conversation held in the native Corsican language. Muller knew he was supposed to call the expulsion of the German army a 'liberation', but he would prefer to call it 'Americanisation'. He looked round at the scantily clad female tourists enjoying their holiday breaks, and the adverts on the posters promoting luxury goods, with disapproval. These seemed virtually indistinguishable from those in other countries and he snorted with derision. He told himself the German occupiers had brought what he felt was much-needed Teutonic discipline to the island.

Now, with the collapse of East Germany, Muller felt it was time to expand his small-scale criminal empire into new areas. He knew that large numbers of diamonds were missing from his wartime adventure and now he was desperate to find them again. He knew that many people, both legitimate and criminal, had been trying to find the missing jewels but he was one of the few people who knew what had happened to them just before Corsica had been liberated in 1943. He should be in the prime position to retrieve the jewels from the bottom of the Mediterranean Sea.

The only other person was that pesky British prisoner of war whom he had co-opted to help him move the heavy jewels. He remembered his name was William Cottrell and Muller would dearly love to know where he was now. Just then, as he was making plans, Muller was stopped by a man in a suit, seeming out of place in the hot weather.

'Mr Muller? I'm with the police. I want a word with you,' the man said, flashing a warrant card.

Muller had not told anyone about his trip to Corsica and studied the man's identification suspiciously. It looked genuine as far as he could tell. 'What do you want?' Muller asked. 'I've only just arrived on the island. I'm here on holiday. I've done nothing wrong.'

The man gave a half-smile. 'The Beast of Bastia claims to have done nothing wrong. That's quite funny.'

Muller looked around to see if they were being overheard. 'Keep your voice down. The war was a long time ago. I've been punished enough for what I did.'

'That's not what half of Corsica thinks. If I told certain people here who you are, you would be lucky to get out alive. But you needn't worry,' the official said, with a cold smile. 'I don't plan to take any action.'

'You don't? Why have you stopped me then?' Muller asked. He stared at the man suspiciously. 'Where is your uniform? What sort of policeman are you?'

'The kind that believes in making money for myself from my job,' the man said, with a slight smile. 'I believe I know why you're here in Corsica. I think you are looking for what they call Rommel's treasure. The authorities are still very interested in it. So am I, but I am concerned in a personal capacity. I feel the two of us can form a profitable partnership. Shall we retreat to that bar and come to an agreement? Or else I can go back to being a police officer, and you will be arrested and probably lynched. Which do you prefer? Why don't I buy you a drink before you decide?'

Muller nodded and the policeman led him into the nearest bar.

'So, what do you want?' Muller asked, once the two men had retreated to a dark corner.

'As I say, I suggest we work together to recover the gold and jewels you lost in 1943.'

'What do you know about that?' Muller asked, looking around to ensure he was not being overheard. 'How do I know I can trust you? You might be really working for the police and recording all this. Why don't I tell you to get lost?'

'You have to make that decision,' the policeman said. 'The alternatives are either allowing me to help you and we each take half of the money you find, or I go back to being a police officer and arrest you. If I make it public that you're back in Corsica, we both know your life won't be worth living.'

'You say you expect half of what we recover. What will you do for that?'

'I will protect you from the law and am happy to crew for you if you hire a yacht. I have some funds that will help fund our expedition.'

'I'll have to see about that. How did you know I would be here?' Muller asked. 'I haven't told anyone about my plans.'

'Being a policeman has its advantages. Your name came up on one of our checks. I decided to keep the information to myself. Of course, if you don't cooperate with me, I will haul you off to a Corsican prison. I am sure I can make up a holding charge.'

Muller stared at the man thoughtfully. He decided he would appear to cooperate with this man for the time being, even though he had no intention of giving him half of what he found. Muller told himself the man's police contacts might be useful for his search. 'There is one thing I want you to help with. One person I need to contact is a British soldier called Lieutenant William Cottrell. He was with me when the jewels were lost, and should know where they are. Can you find him, if he is still alive? One thing I remember is Cottrell had a sergeant called Tony Gash. I could have captured him as well, but he was useful

40

to us, and I let him go free. They may still be in touch with each other.'

'William Cottrell and Tony Gash, you say?' the policeman asked, making a note on his Filofax. 'I have some useful official contacts. I can probably find them. Shall we shake hands on our partnership?'

'I agree. What shall I call you?' Muller asked, as they shook hands.

'Just call me Walter,' the policeman said.

'Walter? But that's not what it says on your warrant card.'

'I suggest we both have good reasons for using false names,' Walter said. 'I don't think you want me to bandy the name of the Beast of Bastia about. How about I call you a German name that would not cause concern?'

'I suppose Schmidt will do, as well as any other German name,' Muller said, after a moment's thought.

The newly named Schmidt and Walter continued their conversation over several drinks.

41

CHAPTER 10

Two days later, the man with the pseudonym Walter was seated at his official desk. He had some spare time and decided to do some work for himself. He assumed his unofficial role of a criminal bent on uncovering some missing Nazi treasure for his own benefit. As agreed with Muller, he wondered the best way of finding the present addresses of William Cottrell, or, failing him, of Anthony Gash, who may still be in touch with Cottrell. There was no guarantee that either was still alive of course, but there was still a reasonable chance that they were.

After a moment's thought, Walter decided to see what use he could make of his official persona. His first step would be to phone up the section dealing with British Army records in Aldershot. After identifying himself in his official role, Walter asked for the records of William Cottrell and Anthony Gash, who were stationed in Corsica in 1943. After a good deal of searching through files, the clerk phoned Walter back.

'Yes, I can see those names on the files, sir,' the clerk said.

'Good, please give me their current addresses.'

'Oh, I can't do that, sir.'

'Why not?' Walter's voice became angry. 'You must know where they live.'

'Yes, of course, we do. We pay their army pensions. But we can't give their addresses out to anyone.'

'But this is an official inquiry. It's your duty to assist me.'

'Perhaps you could write to us and we could forward your letter to them. Then it would be up to them whether they replied to you.'

'No, that won't do. Isn't there any other way I can contact them?'

'Well, unofficially, some old soldiers keep in touch with their old regiments through newsletters and the British Legion. You can find them in libraries or on this new thing called the internet ...'

Walter hung up before the clerk could finish. He could not know the clerk made a note on the file about this unusual request before moving onto other business. Walter used the internet terminal in his office and accessed the website of the British Legion, to which he knew many old soldiers belonged. After failing to find any mention of William Cottrell, he searched for Anthony Gash. After several hours, he found a mention of an Anthony Gash in a newsletter from the Beckenham branch. His regiment was one of those stationed in Corsica during the war. Walter felt hopeful and printed off a picture of Gash at a Remembrance Day procession.

* * * *

The next day, Walter approached the cheap lodging house where he knew Muller was living anonymously.

'Come on, Schmidt,' Walter said, after knocking on the door. He shouted louder when there was no response.

'What do you want?' Muller said, coming to the door. 'I'd almost forgotten that stupid name we agreed on.'

'It may be stupid, but it is a lot safer than your real name. You wouldn't last a day if people knew the Beast of Bastia is in town.'

'Spare me the lecture ... Walter. Don't forget you don't want your real name bandied about, either.'

'Well, I wasn't able to find William Cottrell, but I've discovered a possible mention of a Tony Gash. I've printed off this recent photo. He's a leading member of the local British Legion in a place in England near London called Beckenham,' Walter said, handing over the photo.

Muller took the photo and studied it dubiously. Eventually he nodded. 'Yes, that's him. He was a coward then, and he still looks weak.'

'Are you sure?' Walter asked. 'It is a long time since you last saw him.'

'I'm sure,' Muller said. 'What are we waiting for? Let's fly there. Gash should be able to lead us to Lieutenant Cottrell. I look forward to having an interesting conversation with both of them.'

CHAPTER 11

One evening, a week later, Tony Gash walked to the door of his semi-detached house in Beckenham to answer an aggressive knocking. He was annoyed at being interrupted from watching Coronation Street on the television. He had spent the afternoon drinking with his colleagues at the local British Legion. He had enjoyed regaling them with the, largely imaginary, tales of his wartime exploits.

As he walked along the corridor, he straightened some of his army memorabilia on the wall before he prepared to open the door. He could not imagine who his caller might be, as all his friends would know not to contact him at such an unsociable time. His first guess was that it was Bill Cottrell, returning to see him for some unknown reason.

As Gash opened his front door, an elderly man stood there. Gash realised it was not Bill Cottrell but could not identify him. He gave a welcoming smile, assuming it was some friend, whose face he had forgotten, making an unexpected visit. After a moment, though, recognition set in. Gash's worst nightmare had come to pass.

'Hello, Tony,' Muller said. 'Don't you remember me?'

Gash staggered back as he tried to close the door in his visitor's face.

'Yes, I see you do recognise me,' Muller said, as he stuck his foot into the doorframe, and forced his way into the hallway.

'Muller? Is that you? What are you doing here? I thought you were dead,' Gash said, lamely.

'I am sorry to disappoint you,' Muller said. 'I am very much alive, and I want to renew our … acquaintance.'

'How on earth did you find me?'

'Your name appears prominently in the regimental reunions you have every year. It was not hard to track you down.'

'But what do you want?'

Muller looked at the army memorabilia on the corridor wall. 'I see you pose as a patriotic British soldier,' he said. 'But we both know differently, don't we?'

'I shouldn't have helped you capture Cottrell, but that was a long time ago,' Gash said. 'I was afraid for my life.'

'Indeed so, but I don't think you want your friends in the British Legion knowing how you helped me when I was in the Gestapo all those years ago.'

'So why are you here?'

'Relax! I don't want to harm you. I am trying to contact William Cottrell, your old officer. It occurred to me you would know where he is.'

'I haven't seen Cottrell for fifty years,' Gash lied. 'Why should I know where he is? He might be dead, for all I know.'

Muller approached Gash. He said nothing but merely grabbed Gash and pushed his arm up his back.

'What are you doing? I told you I don't where Cottrell lives,' Gash screamed.

'I don't believe you. I can tell from your eyes you're lying. You were a coward fifty years ago and you're a coward now. For the last time, where is Bill Cottrell?'

'I last saw Cottrell fifty years ago, when you captured him,' Gash lied again.

'Correct, and Cottrell was about to help me escape with a great deal of valuables.'

'What happened then?'

'Our yacht sank near Bastia …' Muller suddenly seemed to realise he was revealing too much information. 'Never mind that, I need to find Cottrell. Where is he?'

Gash, still grabbed from behind by Muller, was about to again

46

deny knowledge of Cottrell's whereabouts. Then a glance at Muller's cruel expression in the mirror in front of him brought all the fears of fifty years before to his mind.

'He visited a while ago. He left a note with his new address. I'll get it for you,' Gash gabbled.

'I see you are seeing sense. You have a minute to give me the information I want,' Muller said.

Gash went back to his sitting room and found the visiting card Bill had left, with the address of his nursing home. He returned to the hall and gave it to Muller, his hands shaking with fear. 'This is all I know,' Gash stammered in fear.

'Yes, that will be fine,' Muller said, taking the card. 'Now, I don't want anyone knowing about my visit, especially not Cottrell. Do I make myself clear? Do you know what will happen to you if you tell anyone about my visit? I may be old, but I should say I still remember the techniques they taught me in the Gestapo. Goodbye … Tony.'

Gash nodded wordlessly and stared after Muller as he left. Gash closed the front door, then staggered back to his armchair, shaking with fear. He wondered what to do. He knew the right action would be to call the police or at least warn Bill Cottrell, but he knew that fifty years after the war, Muller's evil presence was still too strong for him. Gash stared ahead, as broken a man at seventy-three as he had been when he last encountered Muller, when they were both young men.

After the initial shock had left him, Gash thought more about what Muller had said. As someone who had worked in the diamond trade, Gash had heard rumours of Rommel's treasure allegedly being missing since the end of the war. It sounded as if Muller was looking for it, but why did he need to contact Bill Cottrell? Did Cottrell have some information Muller wanted about Rommel's treasure? Gash had many questions but of one thing he was sure. He had spent fifty years hating Felix Muller for the way he had humiliated him during the war, and he hated

Muller even more now. Gash pondered his next steps. He wondered if there was perhaps some way of gaining his revenge on Muller after all these years.

CHAPTER 12

Two days later, Bill Cottrell sat in his retirement home for former police officers in Chiswick. As he dozed, he was thinking of some of the successes in his long and respected career in the Metropolitan Police. Staying in this home for retired officers at little cost was a small perk from his thirty years in the force. He was seated on his own in the games room, which was a welcome respite from the continuous television in the main lounge. He tried to ignore the smell of overcooked cabbage from the kitchen. As he was about to start a jigsaw, a man dressed in blue overalls stood in front of him.

'Mr Cottrell? Or should I say Lieutenant Cottrell?' the stranger said in good English but with a foreign accent.

'Who are you?' Cottrell asked. 'How did you get in?'

'Just call me Walter. Don't call for help. I am here legitimately – people think I'm an electrician.'

'What do you want?'

'I represent a man you used to know,' Walter said. 'Felix Muller.'

Cottrell's eyes widened in fright. 'Muller? Not the Gestapo man in Corsica? I thought he was dead.'

'No, he is very much alive, and he has asked me to find you after all these years. We both know you have information that he needs. He is anxious to recover some diamonds. You know where they are.'

'I don't know what you are talking about,' the old man said, looking around vainly for help.

'I think you do,' Walter said. 'Don't tell anyone about my visit. I will return in a few days to talk some more. Use that time to

49

refresh your memory. If you want to see your pretty granddaughter again, I suggest you tell us the truth when we come back.'

Walter walked away, leaving a stunned Bill Cottrell behind him. Bill picked up his phone. In a terrified voice, he asked his granddaughter to visit him as soon as she could.

* * * *

Later that day, Philippa Cottrell looked at her grandfather in shock. She could not believe what he had just told her. She had arrived at the retirement home, having taken time off, after receiving a call summoning her to talk to her grandfather. He had sounded frightened on the phone, but she assumed something trivial at the retirement home had upset him. She expected she could reassure him, and they could have a relaxed chat talking over their recent holiday in Corsica. Alternatively, she expected they might spend time discussing family history – or comparing police procedure over different eras. She knew her grandfather would spend time telling her how soft he believed the present-day police were. Now the visit had suddenly taken a shocking turn.

'What do you mean you were a thief during the war, Grandad?' she asked, her mouth suddenly turning dry.

'What I say, Philippa love,' the seventy-five-year-old Bill Cottrell continued, his voice still strong. 'Don't look at me like that,' he continued, catching her shocked expression. 'You don't know what things were like back then. I asked you to come to see me, because you'd know what to do about it.'

Philippa looked around to check that they were not being overheard, but the long line of armchairs at the old folk's home for retired police officers was largely empty. She realised that most of the residents were in the dining room, eating their unappetising meals.

'Are you sure you're not exaggerating, Grandad?' she asked,

imagining some trivial misdemeanour that had played on his mind all the years since. 'You were a hero during the war. I've seen the medals they gave you. They don't give those away to thieves.'

'No, I'm sure,' the old man said. 'I could have gone to prison for what I did.'

'Really? And are you sure you want to tell me? Think carefully, Grandad. I'm a police officer, and so were you. I have a duty to report any serious crime, no matter how long ago it was,' Philippa said. 'Perhaps it's best to leave whatever happened in the past. You've led a good life since – you were a fine police officer for thirty years. You don't want your reputation ruined.'

'It doesn't matter much what happens to me or my reputation,' Bill said, giving Philippa a pleading glance. 'I haven't long to live now, but I must tell someone about it. I've received a threatening visit, and I'm worried sick.'

Philippa looked at her grandfather sharply. 'You're saying someone threatened you. Who was it? Was it anything to do with that Amelia woman we saw in Corsica?'

'Shall I start at the beginning?' the old man asked, in a weary voice. 'I'll tell you what happened when I was in Corsica before it was liberated. Then it will all become clear. I've told you parts of it before, but you need to know everything now.'

Philippa nodded. 'If you're sure, you'd better go ahead,' she said.

'Well, it was in 1943.' Bill's eyes focused on a sight somewhere ahead of him. At present, he was staring at a blandly painted wall in his retirement home, but Philippa could tell he was reliving a far distant past, and he was, in his own mind, a young man back in the mountains of Corsica again. Philippa did a quick mental calculation. This was 1994. Her grandfather would have been around twenty-four in 1943.

'I was helping the Free French,' Bill continued. 'As you know, I can speak the language very well. My dad was a wine merchant in Bordeaux before the war, and I picked up French while I was at school there. When the army realised that, I was moved out of the ranks and they gave me a commission. I became a second lieutenant,' he added proudly.

'That must have been quite a dramatic promotion,' Philippa said. 'That doesn't happen very often.' She knew her grandfather came from a cockney working-class family. She found it hard to reconcile him with the stereotype of the public-school educated British Army officer. She wondered if, like some old men, he was exaggerating his past achievements and possibly never became an officer, but she kept that thought to herself. She resolved to let her grandfather tell his story in his own way.

'My sergeant and I were working with the Maquis – you remember I told you that's what they called the Corsican Resistance. I was blowing up bridges and shooting up German staff cars – all that sort of thing. It was fun for a young man, and I was feeling quite pleased with myself. But then one day I suppose I let my guard down. I was meeting Amelia – the woman I saw when I was with you – she was giving us information. As I told you, she was the mistress of Muller, the local Gestapo man.

'I never told you the details of how I was captured. I was just about to blow up the bridge that Muller was supposed to be crossing. If we had been successful, it would have boosted local morale and have disrupted the German troops a lot. I was just about to set off the explosives when Muller and a few of his soldiers appeared, knocked me unconscious, and dragged me away. When I woke up, I was in a German staff car, with the swastika flying from the front, and all the rest of the Nazi paraphernalia. I didn't have the chance to resist. I'm sure they must have known about our plans.'

'Someone must have betrayed you. Do you know who it was?' Philippa asked. 'Perhaps Amelia gave you away.'

'You might be right. When I saw her when you took me to Corte, she denied it and said it was my sergeant who betrayed me, but who knows? I've sometimes wondered if it might have been

Santoni – the Mafia man we saw in his car that day. He always claimed he was cooperating with us to get the Germans out, but he might have betrayed me for money.

'Going back to what happened during the war, all I knew at the time was that I was probably going to be shot – if I was lucky, that is. I wasn't in uniform, so they could torture me. Believe me, you don't want to know what that was like,' Bill added, with a shiver. 'In fact,' he continued, 'the car didn't stop until we arrived at the Gestapo headquarters above Corte – high up in the mountains.

'To my surprise, Muller didn't torture me. He asked me a few questions and drove me to Bastia. When we reached the harbour, he forced me to crew a yacht he had commandeered. He made me load the boat with safe deposit boxes containing jewels. He was hoping to transport them to Italy – whether for his own benefit or for the German regime, I don't know. After a while, the yacht crashed against some rocks. I managed to escape from the wreckage and swam to the land. I assumed Muller had drowned.' Bill then continued to describe the events up to his repatriation by the American forces.

'So, it looks like this Muller man was a common thief. He was probably going to sell them when he reached Italy. He wasn't even loyal to his own side,' Philippa said. 'He sounds like the worst kind of coward. As soon as the going got tough, he planned to sail away and leave his men to face the music and be prisoners of war. Thank God he is dead, now. You said he had drowned, is that right?'

'Yes, I thought he had, but I don't know. Muller was a horrible man – no more than a thug and a criminal. I was just relieved that he wasn't going to torture me there and then.'

Philippa waited to make sure her grandfather had finished his story. It was strange hearing about such dramatic events in the Mediterranean so long ago while sitting in a London retirement home with the smell of overcooked cabbage wafting from the kitchens near where they were sitting. 'But what do you mean you

53

were a thief?' she asked, after a while. 'It sounds to me as if you didn't do anything wrong. Muller had a gun on you the whole time and you didn't have a choice – you were forced to help him. He may have been a thief, but not you. You're still a hero to me.' Philippa paused, then continued when she saw Bill's guilty expression. 'But there's something you haven't told me, isn't there?'

'Yes, you're right, of course. Before the boat sank, I grabbed a bag containing valuables from one of the safe deposit boxes that had broken open and swam with it to the beach. I kept the bag in my pocket while I was being repatriated. On the flight home, I opened it up, and saw loads of diamonds. I didn't know what to do. In the end, I kept them for myself. I know it was wrong. So instead of being a war hero, I'm nothing but a thief.'

'Where are the diamonds now? Have you kept them all these years somewhere?'

'No, I sold them to a trader in Hatton Garden soon after the war. I don't know where they are now.' Bill Cottrell's shame for his theft so many years ago was painful to watch.

'So, you kept the money, even though you knew the diamonds weren't yours? You must have known that was wrong,' Philippa said.

'I suppose I did,' Bill said. 'It seemed too great a temptation.'

'Here's what we must do. We must tell the authorities what we know about where you last saw the diamonds.'

'Isn't it too late now?' Bill asked.

'It's never too late to tell the truth,' Philippa said. 'It might relieve your guilty conscience a little.'

'You sound like a police officer, Philippa,' Bill said, with a half-smile.

'That's what I am – and so were you. You haven't forgotten that, have you?'

'Of course not. I'll cooperate, but the trouble is someone thinks I know where the rest of the jewels are, and a man came around threatening me.'

'Threatening you?' Philippa echoed. 'That's terrible. Could you identify this man?'

'I think so. He seemed young to me – anywhere from thirty to fifty. That seems young when you are my age,' Bill added with a half-smile. 'He spoke good English, but with a slight foreign accent. He said he knew I had stolen the jewels and wanted them back. He threatened to kill me if I didn't agree. That's when I thought of you. I knew you would know what to do.'

'But why should they suddenly contact you now, all these years later? Has something come up?'

'I don't know. Perhaps someone has just found the wreck of the yacht and realised some valuables were missing, but how did they know my name? The man said he represented Muller. Did Muller survive after all? The man was too young to be Muller himself, but could he be an accomplice of his? Did Muller have a son, who wants the money? Perhaps the families of the original owners of the diamonds want them back. If they do, I don't have them.' Bill Cottrell stopped. Philippa suddenly saw him for what he was, a broken man ashamed of his past crime.

'Well, as you know,' Philippa said. 'You should report this visitor to the police. He can't be allowed to threaten you, but if you do that, the police will find out about the diamonds you took. So, are you prepared to face the music, and let the police know you were a thief all those years ago? It's up to you. I could pretend you never told me your story, but you know it's my duty to report it. Why don't you think about it overnight and let me know what you decide? Good night, Grandad. I'll see you tomorrow.'

'I knew you would know what to do, Philippa love,' he said, clasping her hand.

'Yes, try not to worry, Grandad,' Philippa said. She gave a reassuring smile, to try to hide the fact that she was very worried herself.

Philippa led her grandfather up to his room and helped him into bed. She leant over and kissed his forehead. Afterwards, she sat downstairs in the lounge and had a cup of tea to steady her nerves and get her thoughts in order. She had no doubt that, by not returning the diamonds to the authorities, Bill had committed a serious crime in 1943. She realised he was right that, at this late date, she could not imagine what stresses the war had put on him and other soldiers. However, as a police officer, she knew the law would not condone his theft of the valuables, even at this late date.

Philippa pondered what she should do next. She told herself that, as a police officer, she should report her grandfather to the authorities, but she knew she could not do that to the old man. Then, she wondered what to do about the threatening man, and who he was. She hoped he would not return, but somehow doubted her grandfather had seen the last of him.

CHAPTER 13

Later that evening, Bill Cottrell heard the door of his bedroom being opened. Immediately, he sat up in bed. Two men were standing in front of him. 'Who's there?' Bill demanded in a shaky voice.

'Do you remember me, Lieutenant Cottrell?' came a voice in the darkness.

Bill Cottrell looked at the first man and, despite the fifty years since the two men had met, immediately recognised Felix Muller. He was accompanied by the man who had visited Cottrell earlier.

'My God, you're Muller, you should be dead,' Cottrell croaked. 'I thought you drowned long ago.'

'Too right, it's me,' Muller said. 'As you can see, I didn't drown. I've spent many years looking for what you stole from me. Now, I want to know where the diamonds and those missing safe deposit boxes are.'

'What do you mean? What diamonds?' Cottrell tried to look around for some source of help, even though he knew no one was in earshot.

'I don't have time for this,' Muller said, pulling out a gun. 'You stole some valuables from that yacht in Corsica, and I want them back.'

'They were never your property. We both know you stole them.'

'I am not interested in ethics,' Muller said. 'I was going to give you more time, but I saw that pretty granddaughter of yours leaving. She's in the police, isn't she? You don't want her to come to any harm, do you?' He smiled as Bill looked frightened. 'Now, just tell me what you did with the diamonds in those safe deposit boxes and I will leave you alone.'

Cottrell winced. 'Never,' he croaked.

'I may be old, but I have not forgotten my torture skills, Mr Cottrell,' Muller said, then hit Bill with the back of his pistol. Walter stayed by the door to make sure they were not interrupted.

Cottrell let out a groan and started to speak. 'As far as I know, the rest of the jewels are still in that yacht near Bastia. The yacht sank very close to the lighthouse – a few miles west of the harbour. You were unconscious by that stage, so you didn't see where it sank. All I can say is that I guess the yacht sank about a mile and a half from the lighthouse.'

Muller pulled out a detailed map of the seas around Corsica. 'You say you saw a lighthouse. That is here on this map. Tell me where you think the boat sank.'

'You must know. You were there at the time.'

Muller hit Cottrell's face with the gun. 'You know how dark and stormy it was that night, I couldn't see anything. Just answer my questions.'

Cottrell took the map. 'We had just passed the headland when I saw the lighthouse. I'd say we sank about there.' He indicated a point a mile and a half out to sea.

After staring at Cottrell for a few moments, Muller seemed to feel that Cottrell was telling the truth. 'Thank you, Lieutenant. That will be very useful.'

'Will you go away now? I've told you everything I know. You said you'd leave me alone.'

'Not yet. I'd like to know what happened to the jewels you took. I assume you did take some,' Muller added, with a cynical smile.

'Yes, I'm ashamed to say that I did steal some of the diamonds, then sold them after the war,' Bill said, his voice becoming weaker with the pain. 'But, as far as I know, there are plenty still left down there.'

Muller smiled. 'It seems we are both thieves then. Now, I am afraid you have to die,' he said. He looked at Bill's frail body. 'It looks as if you have not much longer to live in any case, so I won't feel too guilty in speeding things up a little. Walter, will you do the necessary? You are younger than me.'

'It would be my pleasure,' Walter said. He raised his right hand and Cottrell uttered a scream. Walter hit Cottrell's neck with a karate chop. Bill gave a pathetic gasp then fell back dead. Walter smiled with satisfaction, then rearranged the body so it looked as though Cottrell had fallen from his bed and died by accident.

'Let's go, now,' Walter said. 'He looks quite peaceful. That should confuse the local police. They'll probably think it was an accident.'

'Well done,' Muller said, hugging Walter. 'That was very efficient – and fun. It brought back memories of the war. I haven't killed anybody for a long time.'

Muller and Walter left the retirement home, happily chatting together. They knew that any staff or residents in the retirement home who saw them would assume they were two local workmen leaving after completing some innocent task.

CHAPTER 14

After leaving her grandfather and returning home, Philippa had mulled over what he had said. She was not sure how much of what her grandfather had said was true. She told herself Bill Cottrell was an old man, and she wondered if he was fantasising in his old age. After a moment, however, she decided it was important to remove him from the retirement home as soon as she could. She wanted to make sure he was not there when the threatening man, whoever he was, returned. Despite what she had told her grandfather, she could not imagine reporting him to the police for a theft he had committed so long ago. The important thing was that he seemed to be in danger where he was, and she wanted him home with her. She decided to take immediate action.

She drove into the retirement home's car park and parked her car. She locked her car door behind her, then froze in shock. She was sure she had heard a scream from the building. It sounded as if it came from an old and frail man, and she felt an instinctive sense of alarm. She ran across the car park and knocked on the front door for at least a minute. Eventually a senior nurse, who looked a caricature of a matron from an old Carry On film, came to open the door.

'Why, Miss Cottrell, I thought you had left. Have you forgotten something? Can I help you?' she asked vaguely.

'Let me in. I'm a police officer. Didn't you hear that scream?' Philippa shouted, as she came into the hall.

'What scream?' the nurse asked, but Philippa had passed her by this time. Without pausing, she rushed up to her grandfather's room. She pushed open the door and stopped in shock. Her grandfather's body was lying lifeless on the floor next to his bed.

Philippa stopped short, but instinctively recalling her police training, she started mouth-to-mouth resuscitation. She stopped when, within a minute, it was clear that the old man was dead.

Philippa turned to the nurse who was standing in a state of shock in the doorway. 'Call the police at once. This is a suspicious death,' Philippa called.

'Are you sure we need the police? Shouldn't it just be an ambulance? It looks like an accident to me,' the nurse said, after checking there were no signs of life.

'No, call the police. I'm worried about this,' Philippa said. After the nurse had gone, Philippa thought about what the woman had said. Philippa realised that like the nurse, any investigator would probably think her grandfather's death was accidental. Then she thought about the state of mind in which she had left him. Philippa knew she would have to give evidence that Bill had been extremely worried about what he had done during the war, which would suggest suicide while the balance of his mind was disturbed. Philippa wondered if Bill could really have decided to kill himself. Was he even fit enough to do it, had he wanted to? She remembered the case of Rudolf Hess, Hitler's deputy leader, who, it was decided, had hung himself at the age of over ninety, but many people thought he had in fact been murdered.

Philippa put such thoughts from her mind, as she told herself she instinctively knew her grandfather had been killed. He had spoken about receiving threats, though she only had his word for them. Why else should he have suddenly become worried about a theft from fifty years ago? She was sure that somehow an unknown person had found out about the theft and believed her grandfather to still have the missing valuables. She immediately visualised giving her evidence to a coroner's court. Even to her own ears, she could see her evidence for murder sounded unconvincing. Even if they did believe her, if she told the authorities everything she had been told, Bill Cottrell's posthumous reputation would be ruined.

Just then, the nurse returned. 'The police said they'd send a car around. You should come away from the body. There is nothing we can do for Mr Cottrell now.'

Philippa reluctantly left the room and closed the door to prevent any contamination of the evidence. 'I'm very worried about this,' she told the nurse. 'Have you seen anyone acting suspiciously in the last hour or so?'

'No, I don't think so,' the nurse said, slowly. 'We did have two electricians looking at the circuits in the corridor, but that was all.'

'What electricians? Are they still here?'

'No, I saw them leave just now.'

'Had you ever seen them before?' Philippa asked.

'No, in fact I remember I was a bit surprised because no one had told me any workmen were expected, and they should have done.'

'Could you describe them?'

'Not really,' the nurse said after a moment's reflection. 'One was youngish. He had on overalls, but he looked a bit smarter than most workmen. He had an air of authority, like a soldier or a policeman, now I think about it. The other was much older. I assumed they were father and son. You get a lot of family firms doing that sort of business.'

'Did they come by vehicle?'

'Yes, I think I saw a van. They should have written their details in the visitors' book. I'll get it for you if you like. But do you want time to recover? It must have been a shock for you finding your grandfather's body. It must have been an accident. Suicide has never happened here before – not in the two years I've worked here. Most of our patients are happy here, but I suppose a few do miss their old lives. Thinking about it, your grandfather seemed a bit worried lately. But I don't know why – he never said anything. Most of our gentleman patients don't like to reveal their feelings. Would you like to come away now?'

'No, I'll stay here,' Philippa said. She heard a male voice calling from the entrance, 'Police here,' and she indicated for the nurse to let the officers in, while she stayed at the scene of her grandfather's death.

'Can you tell me what happened, miss?' one of the constables asked, when he had entered and checked Bill's body.

'This man is my grandfather. I heard a scream and rushed in here. I tried to revive him, but he was dead.'

'And was he well the last time you saw him?'

'He was well, but he was worried over something he had done wrong during the war.'

'Why should he be worried about something that happened fifty years ago?' the officer asked. 'That seems strange. Was he of right mind when you last saw him?'

'Yes, he was fine,' Philippa said. 'I should tell you I'm a detective sergeant in the City of London police, and I am sure he was murdered.'

'That seems quite an accusation, miss … sorry, Sergeant,' the taller constable said after checking Philippa's warrant card. 'Old men fall out of beds all the time. But to be fair to you, we'll wait to see what the police surgeon says.'

'Can I stay with Grandad until the doctor arrives?'

The constable looked at Philippa sceptically. 'Leave it to us, love. We know what we're doing.' He looked startled as the off-duty detective sergeant in front of him burst into tears. 'Tell you what, we'll leave you alone while you say goodbye to your grandfather. You know enough not to touch anything, don't you?'

Once she was alone again with Bill's body, she bent down and kissed his forehead. 'I'll find out who did this, don't worry, Grandad,' she told the corpse.

Philippa left the room a few minutes later, nodding her thanks to the policemen on the door.

CHAPTER 15

Two weeks later, at Chiswick town hall, the coroner cleared his throat at the start of the inquest into Bill Cottrell's death. He was a former family doctor, who obviously enjoyed being a coroner in his retirement. Philippa sitting in the well of the court, decided, before he spoke, that he had an inflated sense of his own importance. The coroner called for the police surgeon to give evidence.

'I confirmed the death of an elderly gentleman at the police retirement home on thirtieth April,' the police surgeon announced. 'The death was obviously suspicious. The body was tied up in the equipment used to lift patients into and out of bed. At first sight, either accidental death or suicide were possibilities. I allowed the body to be moved for examination.

'I carried out the autopsy the following day. I decided death was by asphyxiation. Suicide still seemed the most likely cause of death. The deceased seems to have hung himself from the equipment. I can't see how he could have tied himself up in the apparatus by accident, but it might be possible.'

'Thank you, Doctor,' the coroner said. 'That seems very clear. Does the next of kin wish to raise any matter?'

'Yes, I do,' Philippa said, rising to her feet. 'My grandfather told me he had been receiving threatening visits, which preyed on his mind. Did you consider the possibility of murder?'

The doctor thought. 'I suppose anything is possible, but in view of the deceased's age, he doesn't seem likely to have been murdered. I can't see what motive anyone would have to kill such a harmless old man.'

'It seems clear to me,' the coroner said to Philippa. 'It looks like a case of suicide by hanging. You said yourself your grandfather was upset about something.'

'It wasn't just something,' Philippa said, trying to be an unemotional police officer. 'He said he had been receiving threatening notes about an incident during the war.'

'The police did not find any such correspondence.'

'No, he said he destroyed them.'

'That is a pity. And did he say what the incident was?'

Philippa thought back to her grandfather talking about being a thief during the war and looked round at the handful of people in the public gallery and the court reporter taking notes. She did not wish to ruin her grandfather's reputation and decided to lie. 'He didn't say exactly what the incident was, no, sir,' she said.

'And do you have any comments on the police's view that your grandfather died by suicide?'

'I do not believe my grandfather would have killed himself – he was a brave man, who had not expressed any wish to die.'

The coroner smiled sympathetically in a way that infuriated Philippa. 'Detective Sergeant Cottrell, I understand relatives tend to be opposed to the idea of suicide. But I am obliged to consider the evidence. I rule that the deceased killed himself while the balance of his mind was disturbed.'

Philippa stood up and walked out of the coroner's court, ignoring the shouted questions from the court reporter.

CHAPTER 16

After the inquest, Philippa returned to the retirement home to pick up her grandfather's meagre possessions. A few clothes, books, toiletries, an address book and a post office savings book were all that the old man seemed to have in his possession when he died. It was very hard to believe such a man would have come into contact with the large stash of diamonds he had described to Philippa before he died.

Philippa riffled through Bill's ancient address book. There were names of his friends and former police colleagues that Philippa recognised, and several neighbours and local traders. The only name she did not recognise was that of a man called Tony Gash with a phone number in outer London. Philippa had never heard of him, but she guessed that the most likely way Bill could have met him was in the army. She decided to phone him to invite him to Bill's funeral, and, if possible, to see what this man, whoever he was, knew of Bill's past. After two rings, the phone was answered.

'Gash here,' came an unwelcoming voice.

'Mr Gash, my name is Philippa Cottrell. I believe you knew my grandfather – Bill Cottrell.'

There was a long pause. 'Yes, I knew Bill Cottrell,' the voice said without warmth. Somehow it did not seem to Philippa that Cottrell and Gash were friends.

'I'm afraid he died recently.'

'Oh, had he been ill?' Gash asked.

'No, he died in a mysterious accident.' Philippa decided not to say she believed he had been murdered.

'And why are you telling me this?' Gash sounded abrupt and oddly hostile.

'I am phoning people he knew to invite them to attend his funeral next week, and your number was in his address book,' Philippa said. 'It'll be half-past two on Wednesday at his local church, and I'm laying on a funeral tea in the hotel next door to the church afterwards.'

'Well, if that is all, I must tell you that Bill Cottrell and I used to know each other in the army, but we were not friends,' Gash said. 'I shan't be attending his funeral.'

'I understand, but if you knew my grandfather from the war, I wonder if you can sort out something strange he told me before he died …'

'I don't think so. It was a long time ago,' Gash said, interrupting Philippa. 'Thank you for telling me Bill's dead, Miss Cottrell. I'm sorry for your loss, but I shan't mourn him.'

Philippa heard Gash slam the phone down. She wondered why her grandfather would have bothered to keep the phone number of someone who claimed not to be a friend, and why Gash should sound defensive. In Philippa's experience, most old soldiers were all too happy to talk about the war, and it seemed strange to her that Gash was so reluctant to talk about those days. Philippa put the mystery to one side as she planned her grandfather's funeral.

* * * *

Bill Cottrell's funeral a week later was a small-scale affair. Both of Philippa's parents had died, as had her grandmother, Bill's wife, and Philippa was the only family member present. At the funeral tea, a group of Bill's ex-police colleagues chatted over sandwiches, while they held their pints of beer. Philippa came over to them and they offered polite condolences. They told her some of her memories of Bill during his police career. She felt moved that all these former colleagues had nothing but good things to say about her late grandfather.

Just then, Philippa noticed a man in his seventies dressed in what was obviously his smartest suit, on his own at the bar. She guessed who he was, as she approached him.

'Thank you for coming – Mr Gash, I believe,' she said tentatively.

'How do you do, Miss Cottrell,' Gash said, extending his hand.

'From the way you talked on the phone, I'm surprised to see you here, Mr Gash.'

'Thinking about it afterwards, I realised I may have been harsh on the phone to you – Philippa, isn't it?' Gash said. 'But I wanted to see if any of our colleagues from the army turned up.'

'No, you are the only one,' Philippa replied. 'Now you're here, I'd like to ask you some questions about the war. My grandfather told me some stories just before he died. I'm not sure if his mind was wandering or not. Perhaps you could help me.'

Gash looked at Philippa with suspicion. 'What did Bill tell you?' Gash asked.

'Well, it was about his time in Corsica. Were you with him then?'

'Yes, we were,' Gash replied, smiling slightly for the first time. 'We were young men, driving round, blowing up bridges. It was a great time.'

'But from what you said, it all went wrong between you. What happened?' Philippa asked.

'I'd rather not say. I don't want to tarnish your memory of him,' Gash said, shifting uncomfortably.

'To be honest, I am convinced my grandfather was murdered. I'm interested in finding people with a motive to kill him.' Gash looked at Philippa with a scared expression. 'And you, Mr Gash, seem to have had some grievance against him.'

'You can't think I killed him,' Gash said. 'Who said he was murdered anyway? The coroner said he killed himself.'

'I don't believe that verdict,' Philippa said, moving closer to Gash. 'I'd like to know more about your relationship with my grandfather. How do you know what the coroner decided?'

Gash put his unfinished pint down on the bar. 'I don't wish to discuss this anymore. I know you are a police officer, but this is not the time and you're not on duty. I don't have to answer your questions. I'll be leaving now. Goodbye, Miss Cottrell. Please accept my condolences.'

Philippa stared after Gash as he hurried out of the hotel. She wondered to herself why he felt the need to deny murdering Bill, when she had not even suggested he had. Also, she wondered why Gash had taken the time to find out what the coroner had decided, unless he had some pressing need to follow the case.

Just then, she heard a familiar voice. 'How are things going, Philippa?'

Philippa turned around to see her colleague and friend Detective Chief Inspector David Gould behind her. The two had worked together on several cases. At one stage, they had lived together, but now they were just friendly colleagues who worked in different areas. 'Oh, David, it's good to see you. Thank you for coming,' she said.

'I was sorry to hear about your grandfather, Philippa,' Gould said. 'I wanted to come here in person. He seems to have been a fine police officer. He must have been very unhappy to end his life that way. You must be devastated.'

'My grandfather wasn't unhappy, and he didn't kill himself,' Philippa said, her anger shining through. 'He was being threatened and I'm sure he was murdered. He knew something about some diamonds the Germans lost during the war in Corsica. Someone wanted information and killed him for it. They're probably hunting for the diamonds now. When they find them, they'll be sure to sell them and make a fortune.'

'Are you sure, Philippa?' Gould asked. 'That's not what the coroner decided. It's hard to believe someone from those days would kill your grandfather all these years after the war.'

'Yes, I'm sure someone murdered him,' Philippa said, 'and I aim to find out who it was.'

'Good luck with that, Philippa,' Gould said. 'I'm not sure you're right, though. I know it can be hard to accept a relative has killed themselves, but sometimes it happens. But,' Gould added with a slight smile, 'if someone suddenly appears with a suspicious load of diamonds, we will know where they came from.'

* * * *

An hour after leaving the funeral, Tony Gash entered his house in Beckenham, and sat down with a sigh of relief. He admitted to himself that he had found Bill Cottrell's funeral unsettling and his granddaughter very scary. For some reason he imagined she had followed him all the way home. He caught sight of himself in a mirror. He realised how he must appear to Philippa – a broken man, and one with some guilty secret about her grandfather.

He ran through the last angry conversation he had a few months ago with Bill Cottrell. Bill had accused him of betraying him to the Gestapo back in 1943. Gash had denied it, of course, but he could tell Bill had not believed him. Gash was worried that Bill might tell some of their old colleagues about his treachery. At least now Bill was dead, that was no longer possible.

Gash then recalled what Muller said in that terrifying visit. Although he tried to make excuses for himself, Gash knew that he had betrayed his old officer twice – once during the war and again more recently. Felix Muller had turned him into a traitor, and Gash hated him for it. Gash told himself there must be some way of exacting vengeance on the elderly German. He wondered where Muller was now. From what he had said, he gathered that Muller was about to undertake work to recover some ill-gotten gains that were still missing in Corsica.

Gash looked at old photos of himself in uniform, hanging on his wall. He enjoyed regaling his British Legion friends with his imaginary military successes. However, he had to acknowledge to himself he had been, in all honesty, a sorry apology for a soldier back then. He knew he should not have told Muller what

Bill Cottrell was planning in 1943 and should have resisted Muller's threats when he visited recently.

Gash fantasised that perhaps he could redeem himself by killing Muller. He would enjoy seeing Muller suffer for what he had done. He did not know exactly where Muller was now, but, from what he had said, he guessed he was somewhere in Corsica, probably in Bastia. Gash decided he would stand up to the elderly German for the first time in his life. He resolved to buy a plane ticket to Corsica to see what harm he could do to Muller's plans. At last, he had a plan to revenge himself against Muller. He saw his reflection in a mirror and suddenly felt that he was standing straighter. For the first time in ages, Tony Gash felt he had recovered some of his pride.

CHAPTER 17

A month after Bill Cottrell's murder, Muller found himself looking at a yacht advertised for hire in Bastia harbour. The vessel looked suitable and he knew Walter had provided enough funds to hire her for a month, which he felt would be adequate. With the information Muller had extracted from Bill Cottrell, he was confident he would be able to retrieve his share of Rommel's treasure. He looked back fondly to Bill's cries of anguish and smiled to himself. He told himself he had quite enjoyed torturing Bill Cottrell and was looking forward to putting the newfound knowledge he and Walter had extracted from the old man to profitable effect.

But Muller knew he needed a crew, as the yacht would be too large to manage on his own. Walter obviously expected to be one member of the crew, but two men would not be enough. At least one more crew member was needed, but they must not be too honest or too inquisitive for his purposes. Muller knew he had to look around for a third crew member.

He thought back to his wartime experiences here in Corsica. Was there anyone alive who would still help him? He knew as well as anyone that, as an ex-Nazi occupier, there were many people who would be happy to see him dead. He wondered if he could hire a member of some criminal gang to help him. He remembered Santoni from the war – the man who had initially revealed Bill Cottrell's whereabouts back in 1943. But any member of the Mafia or similar criminal gang would want a large part of any treasure Muller might find. Alternatively, Santoni, or whoever may have replaced him, might refuse to cooperate and decide to hand him over to the authorities or to the general public, who would probably treat him even worse.

The only possible person to help him would be the woman with whom he had an affair for most of the time he was in Corsica. Amelia Luri should still be alive, he told himself. He did not know what her reaction would be to his sudden reappearance on the island. Muller realised she probably still hated him. No doubt she had only slept with him out of fear of his authority and the generous black-market goods he had supplied her with, but still he thought there was a chance she would help him. In any case, he was sure she was still too frightened of him to betray him to the authorities. He remembered where she lived. Amelia came from an old Corsican peasant family and he felt she probably would not have moved far since the war. He decided to pay her a visit.

* * * *

The next day, Muller found a suitable hiding place outside Amelia's old house. On the first morning, after a long wait, he saw an old woman leave the house to go shopping. She was dressed in black, in line with Corsican tradition, and her hair was grey. He kept a safe distance, but as soon as he saw her face, he had no doubt it was his former mistress. His first instinct was to approach her, but he knew she would probably scream for any family members she might have for help. Muller told himself he did not want to encounter any husband or partner Amelia may have acquired since he left Corsica fifty-one years before.

After watching Amelia's house all day and not seeing any sign of any other person, Muller decided she seemed to be living alone. He resolved it was safe to approach her directly. He walked up the path and knocked on the door. After a couple of minutes, the old woman he thought he remembered came to the door and stared in shock.

'Hello, Amelia,' Muller said.

The woman seemed baffled, but then grew faint. 'My God, Felix, is that you? How can you still be alive? Everyone told me you were dead.'

'As you see, I am very much alive. May I come in?'

'Yes, come in, quickly,' Amelia said. 'I don't want the neighbours to see you. What have you been doing all these years? How are you still alive? When the Americans couldn't find your boat, I assumed you'd drowned.'

'Assumed or hoped?' Muller asked with a wry smile, as he entered the house.

'Both really. We were never really lovers, were we, Felix? You must know I only stayed with you to save my life.'

'Yes, I know you never loved me. I may be many things, but I've never been a fool. You had a husband, I seem to remember. What happened to him?'

'He died ten years ago,' Amelia replied. 'Don't be sorry. He used to beat me because of you. I'm better off without him.'

'Did you have children?'

Amelia paused. 'No, I've never had children. Why have you come back? Don't you realise how dangerous it is for you to be seen, after what you did to the people here? Don't you know how everyone hated you during the war? Don't you know what the locals did to people they thought were collaborators?'

'I've seen the pictures of the women in Paris after we'd left, and I'm sorry. I really am. How bad was it for you?'

Amelia shuddered as she thought back to the time she had been shaved, stripped naked and paraded through the streets like an animal, while her neighbours, led by Santoni, the local Mafia chief, jeered at her. 'It was bad enough, but you don't want to know about that. What do you think the locals would do to Nazis like you if they knew you were here?' she asked.

'I know what they would want to do to me. I'm trusting you not to give me away,' Muller said, keeping his eyes fixed on Amelia's face.

'So, what are you doing here now?' she asked, looking ever more worried.

Muller drew a deep breath. 'There is a large stash of diamonds that I was forced to leave behind at the bottom of the sea before I was evacuated back in 1943. I've hired a yacht in Bastia and I'm looking for help in getting the diamonds back.'

'Why are you telling me? Why should I help you?'

'For one thing, if you helped me, there would be money in it for you – a great deal of money,' Muller said. 'You must admit I was always very generous to you.'

Amelia snorted with derision. 'I could get more money by handing you over to the police. I'm sure they'd still be interested in finding you. Or I could tell the press – they would pay me a lot of money. I don't think you would enjoy having your picture in the local paper.'

'I've hired a yacht. I need a crew to help me find the diamonds and gold I left here. I've recently come into more information that should help me find it. Do you know anyone who would help me and keep their mouth shut about it?'

Amelia thought for a moment then stood up. 'No, I don't know anyone who would help you. Now, go away, Felix, and don't come back.'

Muller nodded his understanding. 'If you need me, you can find me near Bastia harbour. I hope you won't regret turning me down, Amelia,' Muller said before leaving the house. 'Don't tell anyone about this visit, will you? It's best for you if you keep it secret. I may be an old man now, but you know you don't want to cross me.'

Amelia stood up and pointed toward the door. 'Get out, Felix, and don't ever come back. You say I don't want to cross you, but, believe me, you don't want to know what I will do to you if I ever see you again.'

Muller stood up. 'Goodbye, Amelia. Think about what I said, won't you?' He left the cottage, slamming the door behind him, without waiting for a reply.

Amelia looked out of the window, making sure Muller had indeed left, before she sat down in an armchair, shaking in shock at the unexpected visit. After a moment, a man aged about fifty came out of one of the bedrooms in Amelia's house. 'Who was that man, Maman, and what did he want?' he asked.

Amelia gave a lengthy sigh. For the first time in fifty years, she was about to tell her son the truth about the dark wartime years. 'Paulu,' she said, calling him by the Corsican name she had christened him with. 'That man is Felix Muller. People called him the Beast of Bastia.'

'I've heard of him. He was the worst of the Nazis on the island. What did he want? I thought he was dead.'

'So did I. But he has come back. And I need to tell you something,' Amelia said, then paused before betraying her secret. 'Paulu, I denied it to him just now, but I think Felix is your father.'

'Muller is my father?' Paulu stared in shock. 'What are you talking about? I always thought Papa was my father.'

'Yes, it was easier to tell everyone that, but the truth is I lived with Felix during the war. He may have been your father. I never loved him – in fact, I hated him – but he stopped me from going hungry.'

Paulu looked aghast at his mother for a long time. 'Let's get this clear, Maman. For the first time in my life, after all this time, I've found out my father was a Nazi. That must be why Papa used to treat me so badly. What's worse, my mother was a traitor who sold her body for food.'

Amelia replied in a broken voice. 'I'm sorry, Paulu. If I had my life to live again, I would do it all differently. I wasn't a traitor though. I used to tell the Resistance what Felix was doing. There was a British officer called Bill who I used to supply with information. I saw him recently, when he came to see me. He thought I had betrayed him that last day, but I told him it wasn't me. I'm sure his sergeant was a traitor and he betrayed him to Felix.'

'Did you sleep with the British guy as well?' Paulu asked, with contempt.

'No, of course I didn't. He was too much of a gentleman.'

Paulu picked up his jacket. 'I can't take much more of this. I'm going out. Why did Muller come to see you today anyway? I couldn't hear everything he said.'

'He is hanging around Bastia looking for help in recovering some diamonds he says were lost at the end of the war.'

'Well, I'm going to drive to Bastia to tell Muller what I think of him.'

'No, don't. You don't know what sort of temper he has ...' Amelia started to say, then stared sadly after Paulu as he stormed out, slamming the door of their shared house.

CHAPTER 18

After leaving Amelia's house, Muller had rushed to his car before driving dangerously fast down the steep roads to Bastia. He decided to take a different approach to recruiting a third crew member. Wandering around the town, he spotted a rundown bar close to the harbour. He told himself the sort of crew he was likely to be able to afford would probably spend their spare time in such a place. He was confident he would not be recognised as an outsider. He had acquired a reasonable French accent during the war and did not think he looked out of place. He walked in, ordered a drink, and found a quiet corner to observe the comings and goings of the regulars, unnoticed.

Muller planned to stay most of the evening and see what he could learn. He enjoyed his cognac in peace for around half an hour. Suddenly a man he did not recognise came into the bar and walked over to him.

'Mr Muller, I believe?' Paulu said.

Muller looked round startled. 'Who are you? What do you want?'

'Let's just say I know who you are and what you're doing here. You're the Beast of Bastia, aren't you?'

Muller looked around to make sure they were not being overheard. 'Go ahead but keep your voice down.'

'First of all, you want me to keep quiet. A lot of people lost relatives to the Nazis. If they knew who you are, you wouldn't leave this town in one piece.'

Muller looked at Paulu, who, although a stranger, looked vaguely familiar. 'If you know so much about me, you will know

I'm not someone you want to cross. Now go away, before I show you what I am capable of.'

Paulu smiled. 'I'm guessing you are looking for someone to help you find some missing treasure.'

Muller stared at him, too stunned to speak.

'Yes, I heard about what you said to Amelia Luri. She is my mother. She lied when she told you she had no children. You should know I believe I am your son.'

Muller looked at Paulu and felt he could see a resemblance to both himself and Amelia. He shrugged with indifference. 'So, she lied and you're my son. I believe you, but I am not what you call the paternal type. I don't have any money for you. If you have any sense, you will leave now and forget you ever saw me.'

'I'm not looking for a handout. If you are looking for crew for your yacht, why not choose me? I make a living out of crewing for rich men. Why not keep it all in the family?'

Muller paused, then after a while, he nodded agreement. 'I suppose you could crew for me, if you do have experience,' Muller said, keeping his eyes fixed on Paulu. 'I don't mind employing you, but you should know this is strictly business. I will pay you a generous wage, but, if you betray me, I will kill you whoever you are – even if you are my son.'

Paulu stretched out his hand. 'I won't betray you. That's all agreed. I say we have a deal ... Papa,' Paulu said, and after a pause the two men shook hands.

* * * *

Later that evening, after Paulu had gone back home, Muller left the bar, then walked along the harbour to return to his lodging house. As he stopped to take a key from his pocket, a young woman approached him.

'Felix, I've been looking for you,' she said. Muller was at first baffled, then, through his alcoholic haze, recognition dawned. It was Zoe, the girlfriend he thought he had left behind in Berlin.

'Zoe, is it you?' he asked. 'What are you doing here? How did you find me?'

'I guessed you might be here. You've often talked about Bastia,' Zoe said. 'I thought I would have a little holiday to see how you are.'

'But you have to go back to Berlin. It's dangerous for you here.'

'Why should it be dangerous for me here, Felix?' Zoe asked, suspiciously. 'It's a lovely peaceful holiday island. You are on holiday here, aren't you?'

'I can't talk about it now.'

'I've picked up some leaflets on the history of Corsica since I've been here. There's quite a lot about the mystery of Rommel's treasure in them. Lots of people think it sunk in the sea near here. You're trying to find some of that money, aren't you?'

'For God's sake go back to Berlin, Zoe,' Muller said, turning to walk away. 'You don't know what it's like in Bastia. It's not safe for you here.'

'I'm not a fool, Felix. I know what you are up to,' Zoe screamed after him. 'Don't think you can leave me behind with no money.'

'I left enough money for you in our flat. Goodbye, Zoe,' Muller said, turning to leave. 'I can't do anything more for you.'

Left behind on the quayside, Zoe looked at the expensive yachts around her. She could see this was a completely different world from the old Communist East Berlin where she had grown up. There must be some way of making a profit from her visit to Corsica. She was sure there was some way of extracting money from their owners, who would not miss losing a few thousand francs.

CHAPTER 19

The following day, Zoe sat at a café on Bastia harbour, drinking a coffee. She looked at some fading press cuttings in her possession that Muller thought he had kept hidden. During her time with him, she was always mindful that he might run out on her, and she had kept an eye on his papers. These mostly related to expeditions to recover Rommel's treasure over the years. For some reason they had excited Muller's curiosity.

One cutting in particular described how a rich man called Edwin Link was looking for the lost treasure. Zoe had heard his name mentioned as she had walked around Bastia harbour. He apparently owned the huge yacht she had seen moored nearby. Link obviously had plenty of money to spare, and Zoe would be happy to take some from him.

Her plan was to pretend to know the whereabouts of the treasure that she would promise to reveal in return for a large amount of cash. That could work, she told herself, but she was scared Link would want some sort of revenge once he found she had no idea where it was. Perhaps just telling him that Felix Muller was around might be enough information to whet Mr Link's appetite.

Zoe was sure that the largest yacht on the harbour belonged to Link and she walked up to it. As she stood on the quayside, Zoe looked up at the huge vessel, and gasped. She had never seen, or even imagined, such a yacht. Gazing around, she walked up to the gangway and called to the crew member waiting at the top.

'I want to see Mr Link,' she called.

The crew member looked at Zoe up and down with contempt. Zoe was too used to such looks from passers-by to be offended.

'Mr Link won't want to see you,' he said. 'He doesn't need women like you. Just go away.'

'I have information that he will be interested in,' Zoe shouted back. 'I know he is looking for Rommel's treasure,' she said.

'Everyone knows that,' the crew member called back, with a laugh.

'I know where the treasure is.'

'How? You weren't even born when it went missing.'

'Just tell Mr Link I know where Felix Muller is,' she said.

'Felix who?'

'Just tell him,' Zoe called.

The crew member stared at Zoe, then gruffly told her to say where she was. After a couple of minutes, he returned.

'Follow me. Mr Link will see you,' the crew member said, not bothering to hide his surprise. After Zoe had climbed the gangway, he led her along the oak-panelled corridor to Link's office. She saw an elderly man wearing a naval blazer, and the pampered air of the very rich. The wealthy Texan did not bother to rise.

'Are you Mr Link?' she asked.

'Yes, what do you want? I am very busy,' Link said, without looking at Zoe.

'I believe you have heard of Felix Muller. He was responsible for losing Rommel's treasure that you are looking for,' Zoe said.

'Felix Muller is dead,' Link said. 'Why are you wasting my time?'

'I've been living with Felix for the last few years in Berlin,' Zoe said. 'He left not long ago, and I've just seen him here in Bastia.'

'If this is true, why are you telling me?'

'He left me behind in Berlin and I need money,' Zoe said, looking around at the palatial cabin. 'Somehow, I think you have plenty of spare cash. I could tell you where he is for a few thousand francs.'

Link smiled. 'Well, your story's very interesting. I'm very

grateful.' Suddenly his demeanour changed. 'Show her out,' Link called to his crewman.

'What about my money? You have plenty,' Zoe screamed, as she was forcibly escorted off Link's yacht. The crewman deposited her on the quayside. By this time, she had reverted to her native language, as she shouted unintelligible threats in German aimed at Link and his yacht.

CHAPTER 20

The next evening, Muller walked out along the quayside in Bastia. He was in a good mood as he felt confident that his project to retrieve Rommel's diamonds was on course for success. He had the information on the location of the wrecked yacht that he had extracted from Bill Cottrell under torture before he and Walter and killed him. Now with a yacht hired, and Walter and Paulu as crew members, on a trip to recover the treasure, he was feeling that things were about to go well.

As he passed through a particularly dark alley back to his hotel, Muller found himself suddenly grabbed from behind. It happened too suddenly for Muller to resist – the assailant was obviously a strong young man and Muller was no match for him. As he was considering whether to give the assailant money to let him escape, a man of about Muller's age emerged from the darkness, holding a large knife.

'Herr Muller, do you remember me?' he said.

Muller was baffled at first, then, through the years, he remembered when he had last seen the man in front of him. 'My God, you're Santoni,' he gasped.

'Exactly so. I see you know my name, but do you remember what I do?'

Muller hesitated. 'You used to help your father run the mafia around here. I guess you've taken over by now.'

'You guess right – and how do you know me?'

'What's all this about?'

'Answer the question,' Santoni said, and he nodded for the man behind Muller to pull his arm higher up behind his back.

Muller screamed with pain. 'You know how. We worked

together. You told me about that British soldier, and I captured him.'

'I know that, Herr Muller, and you know that,' Santoni said, 'but, as far as everyone else in Corsica is concerned, I am a patriotic Frenchman and worked hard to liberate Corsica. I was a loyal member of the Resistance, and never cooperated with the Nazis,' he paused. 'Do you understand me? Now do you know who I am?'

Muller hesitated while he calculated the right answer to make Santoni release him. 'I don't know you, Mr Santoni. I have never met you before.'

'That's correct, and don't tell anyone else otherwise. Now, tell me, why are you here in Corsica?'

'I'm just on holiday, Mr Santoni,' Muller mumbled, keeping an eye on Santoni's knife.

'Good, just make sure you leave soon. I don't want to see you here again.'

'Yes, of course, Mr Santoni.'

Santoni nodded to his henchman, who reluctantly let Muller go. Muller moved away as quickly as his seventy-five years-old legs would carry him.

* * * *

The next day, Muller, Walter and Paulu walked along the jetty in Bastia and approached the yacht that Muller had hired to search for Rommel's treasure. He felt that she was now adequately provisioned for his search operation. He idly looked across at the mammoth luxury yacht that he knew was owned by the American millionaire Edwin Link, moored at the other end of the quay. From the press cuttings that Zoe had since found, Muller had heard that Link spent every summer looking for Rommel's treasure, so far without success. Muller sneered to himself as he reflected that his own search operation was likely to be far more successful than Link's, thanks to the extra information he had extracted from Bill Cottrell before he and Walter had killed him.

Muller had a childish urge to make a mocking gesture at Link's yacht. He looked up and saw an elderly man with a captain's cap peering down at him. He suddenly had an instinctive feeling that the man, presumably Edwin Link himself, had recognised him. Muller pulled down his own cap before climbing onto his own yacht. He had no wish to be recognised before he had found the valuables he was looking for.

'Hey, I know you,' came a call from the ship's captain. 'You're Muller, aren't you?'

'Let's go. We don't want to be late,' Muller called to Walter and Paulu, who were ready to sail away. The yacht set sail and headed to the area that Bill Cottrell had marked on the map while being tortured. Muller smiled. He felt sure this was an area that no other treasure hunter had searched before. He did not see Edwin Link's yacht sail discreetly after him.

* * * *

Muller had not seen Zoe follow him from his hotel that morning. From the jetty, Zoe saw Muller approach a yacht with two other men and sail off. She heard a muffled shout from the larger yacht moored nearby but could not understand what was being said. At a loose end, she walked around the picturesque harbour and admired the expensive yachts. She wondered what Muller was doing in such opulent surroundings.

After a while she sat down in a nearby café. Despite what she had told Muller, she did not really know what he was up to. Knowing his prime motivation was money, she was sure that he would return from his journey richer than before. She decided to stay where she was until Muller sailed back. Then she would see what other way there was to extract money from him.

* * * *

From the jetty, the elderly Englishman gazed at Muller with hatred as he sailed away on his yacht. Tony Gash reminded himself how badly he had been humiliated twice in his life by Felix Muller. He wished there was some way he could gain his revenge by killing the man, without being caught. Gash had travelled to Bastia, guessing that this was where he was headed, and found Muller after a couple of days' search. He assumed that Muller had some plan to recover the treasure that he had left behind in 1943.

Gash asked himself what his aim was in following Muller; all he knew was there must be some way his humiliation could be avenged. He had heard the expression 'even a worm will turn' and felt it applied to himself. In the fantasy he developed in his head, he would enjoy making Muller suffer before he killed him. He wondered to himself how he could make it happen.

A few feet away, Gash saw a local woman whom he felt he recognised. Yes, he told himself, she had obviously aged a good deal, but he was sure it was Amelia, Muller's mistress. She seemed to recognise him as well. He knew, from Bill's visit, that Amelia had somehow guessed about his treachery in 1943 and he did not wish to see her again. Gash walked slowly away, still planning his revenge on Felix Muller.

* * * *

Muller stood on the deck of his hired yacht not far from the lighthouse on the shore, then studied his map. He picked out the shaky pencil mark made by Bill Cottrell while he was being tortured. Muller smiled with excitement.

'This looks to be the place,' he said.

'Let's go diving then,' Walter said. 'Lower the anchor,' he called.

'Sure thing,' Paulu said from the stern of the yacht, as he lowered the anchor into position.

After a few hours diving, Walter brought an old safety deposit box to the surface. Muller took it, as Walter looked on in excitement. Muller took a chisel and forced open the lock. The two men were struck silent as they peered at the diamonds inside.

After fifty-one years the jewels were covered with silt and seaweed, but the men knew they could easily be cleaned and sold. Muller and Walter gave each other a congratulatory hug. Walter dived down again and picked up two more boxes.

By the end of the day, Muller had decided he had found all the treasure he suspected to be in the sea. The crew of three sailed the yacht back to the harbour and moored her. In a good mood, he called out to the man he believed to be his son. 'Hey, Paulu,' he called. 'We've done it.' Muller held out his arms for the expected hug of congratulation. Before he could say anything else, a harpoon entered his chest and Felix Muller collapsed dead.

Several diamonds dropped out of Muller's dead hand and scattered over the deck. The murderer picked them up and put them in his pocket. He smiled with satisfaction, as he kicked Muller's body into the sea. He knew the jewels should fetch a good price on the London diamond market.

From the shore, Zoe had seen the murder of Muller taking place. She did not know the murderer's name, but could guess that, somehow, the missing diamonds – part of Rommel's treasure – were at the heart of it. She knew her civic duty would be to report what she had seen to the local police. She also felt that, with her lengthy crime record, they would be very unlikely to believe she was an innocent witness. Also, Zoe knew that, if she reported it to the police, there would be a good chance the murderer, whoever he was, would find out she was a witness, and would kill her as well. Zoe decided to keep quiet about having seen Muller's murder, biding her time until she could find some way of making money out of it. She entered a café on the quayside to await developments. She did not initially take much notice of the elderly Englishman sitting near her.

CHAPTER 21

It took around a quarter of an hour before Muller's death was reported to the police. A Danish tourist walking by spotted Muller's corpse floating face down in Bastia harbour with blood seeping out and discolouring the water. A uniformed gendarme asked a local fisherman to pull it out, and onto the edge of the harbour.

It was not immediately obvious to the authorities that the death was murder. Many people die accidentally in the sea each year, and the blood could have been caused by a fall onto a rock. When the gendarme turned the body over, and he saw the harpoon in Muller's chest, he set up the required procedure for a possible homicide.

The gendarme searched Muller's pockets and pulled out a German passport. When he recognised the dead man's name, he exclaimed in surprise and radioed for a senior detective to arrive as soon as possible.

* * * *

An hour later, Tony Gash was still in the café, looking at the developments following the murder through the large window. He watched fascinated as Muller's dead body was being carried away by the police. He was not sure if the death of the man he most hated in the world was as satisfying as he had hoped it would be. Now the old Nazi was dead, Gash felt he could move on with his life. He had just decided to catch the next plane back to England when the voice of an elderly Corsican woman startled him.

'Hello, Tony,' Amelia's voice made Gash jump. He immediately recognised her but had no wish to talk to her.

'Pardon, madame,' he replied, trying to leave. 'You have made a mistake.'

'Don't you remember me?' Amelia asked.

'Amelia? Is that you?' Gash said, acting suitably nonplussed. 'It's been a long time. I'd love to talk, but I have to go.'

'Would you rather talk to me or to the police?' Amelia asked.

'Police? What do you mean?' Gash replied.

'Won't you buy me a coffee, Tony? We could talk about old times.'

When the two were seated with coffees in front of them, Gash turned to Amelia. 'So, how have you been?' he asked.

Amelia shrugged. 'I've survived. The years after the Liberation were the worst. Do you know what my neighbours did to people like me?'

'I've seen the pictures of women being lynched. It looked horrible,' Gash said.

'Yes, they called me a traitor,' Amelia said, as Gash shrugged. 'But I didn't betray Bill Cottrell, did I? We both know it was you.'

Gash looked scared. 'That's rubbish,' he said. He looked at Amelia and was sure that he would never see her again. Suddenly, something inside him broke and he decided to tell her the truth. 'Yes, you're right, of course. It's the worst thing I've ever done. It was to save my life, when Muller threatened to kill me, but that does not make it any better. I betrayed my country and my friend. I'm sorry for what I did, but I can't put it right now.'

'Does Bill know about it?'

'He never knew. We used to send each other friendly Christmas cards, but after a few years, we lost touch. I could never face meeting him. He came to see me, after he visited you, you know. Now his granddaughter's told me he's dead. I went to his funeral.'

Amelia fell silent for a few moments. 'I'm sorry to hear Bill's dead. I expect it was through natural causes. He didn't look well when I saw him earlier this year.'

'No, the inquest said he killed himself, but I'm sure he was murdered by Muller. He came to my house and forced me to reveal Bill's address.'

'So, you betrayed Bill Cottrell a second time,' Amelia said, her voice laced with contempt. 'How can you live with yourself?'

'Muller forced me to tell him Bill's address. He would have killed me otherwise. I feel guilty about it.'

'Is that why you killed Felix?'

'What are you talking about?' Gash looked aghast at Amelia.

'I saw you in the harbour earlier. I think you killed him.'

'I didn't kill Muller,' Gash gasped in shock. 'I'm glad he's dead, but I didn't kill him. What makes you think I did?'

'Let's see how it looks, shall we? You came to Corsica – for the first time in fifty years, I guess. While you are here, the man you have every reason to hate is murdered. Felix threatens your life and now he's been killed himself, while you are nearby. It doesn't look good for you, does it?'

Gash looked frightened. 'You won't tell anyone I was here, will you?' After a moment, he continued. 'One moment. Why are you here? You hated him as well. You could have killed him as easily as I could. If the police interview me, I'll point them in your direction. I suggest we both keep this chat secret.'

Amelia uttered some French oath, incomprehensible to Gash, and stormed out of the café. Gash sat back in a state of shock and mulled over their conversation. Suddenly a young blonde woman joined his table.

'That was an interesting conversation,' Zoe said, in her German accent. 'It made me glad I learned English at school.'

Gash looked at her blankly. 'Who the hell are you? What do you want?'

Zoe smiled without mirth. 'Never mind who I am. The important thing is I saw the murder of Felix Muller this afternoon. So did you, according to that lady.'

Gash gazed at her. 'You knew Muller? Was he a friend of yours?'

'Felix Muller didn't have friends, but I knew him well enough. Now Felix is dead, let's just say I am sure the police would be interested in the conversation I overheard.'

'I didn't kill Muller,' Gash said, lamely.

'Maybe not, but that lady seemed to think you did,' Zoe said, with a cunning smile. 'The police would detain you for a long time if I tell them what you and she were talking about. There's no way they will let you leave the country.'

'What do you want?' Gash gasped.

'Why don't you just give me the money in your wallet?' Zoe asked with a cold smile. 'Then I'll forget I ever saw you and what I just heard.'

Gash glared at her, then pulled a few hundred francs from his wallet and threw them on the table. 'Now, go to hell,' he said, storming out.

'Thank you, sir. It was a pleasure doing business with you,' Zoe muttered to herself. She counted the money Gash had given her and smiled. She estimated that it should be just enough to fly her back to Berlin and away from any awkward police questioning. She left the café and prepared to make her way to Bastia airport.

CHAPTER 22

A week later, the murderer of Felix Muller walked through Hatton Garden. He had the first few of Muller's diamonds in his pocket. He knew most of the world's diamonds passed through this small part of London. He wanted a good price for this haul, without being too greedy and having someone alerting the police. He told himself there would be plenty of time to sell the rest of his hoard in due course.

In the distance, he saw a small diamond trader called Samuelson's and decided that would do to start with. Then he would try other traders with a diamond each to avoid scaring them too much. He rang the doorbell of the trader he had spotted, then waited for someone to answer. After a minute or so, an elderly man came to the door and looked at his caller with suspicion.

The murderer displayed a professional charming smile. 'Good morning, sir,' he said. 'How are you today? Please can you give me a quote for some diamonds I have to sell.'

Mr Samuelson stared at the man in shock. Painful memories came to the old man as he tried not to faint.

* * * *

The next day, Detective Chief Inspector David Gould climbed the stairs of the same Victorian building in Hatton Garden. He idly made a note of how many diamond traders he could see in this neighbourhood and was soon counting around fifty. He knocked on the door of a second-floor establishment and, after some time spent drawing back several bolts, an elderly man came to the door and gazed at him.

'Mr Samuelson? I'm DCI Gould of the City of London police,' Gould said, displaying his warrant card, which Samuelson studied suspiciously. 'I came about your call to the station. The officer who spoke to you asked me to see you.'

'Ah, yes, come in, Inspector,' Mr Samuelson said, ushering Gould into his dusty workshop. Gould gasped as he took in the contents. He found it hard to believe that such antique equipment could exist side by side with the modern skyscrapers outside. 'Take a seat, Inspector Gould,' Mr Samuelson said, indicating a rickety-looking wooden chair. Gould gave it a discreet dusting before sitting down.

Gould decided not to correct Mr Samuelson's downgrading of his actual rank and took out a notebook. 'I have the constable's notes, of course, sir, but please tell me in your own words what happened,' he asked.

'I had a strange visit yesterday,' Mr Samuelson replied. 'It was what you would call very … unsettling,' he continued, having obviously searched for the correct English word. His middle-European accent grew more pronounced as he relived the visit. Gould assumed Samuelson was Jewish because of his name and wondered what his history might have been. Gould felt sure that Samuelson had undergone some traumatic experiences during the war that had made him live as an exile in London.

'Please don't upset yourself, Mr Samuelson,' Gould said, preparing to take notes. 'Just tell me what happened as calmly as you can.'

'Well, this man came in and wanted to sell a diamond. He showed it to me. Very valuable, it was. Good quality merchandise.' Mr Samuelson paused.

'You are a diamond trader, Mr Samuelson. Surely that must happen a lot.'

'Yes, but this was different.'

'Perhaps if you tell me why there was a problem,' Gould prompted. He was becoming exasperated at Mr Samuelson's hesitations, but he had many years of experience in encouraging distressed witnesses to record their experiences. Trying to hurry them up merely slowed the process in the long term. He knew it was best to wait patiently for the old man to continue his story in his own way.

'I asked him where it came from,' Samuelson continued. 'I always wish to know the provenance of any diamond I handle, but he wouldn't tell me. That's when I became suspicious.'

'Did he seem like the sort of man who would have diamonds legitimately? Or did he seem like a crook?'

'Not just a normal crook.'

'How do you mean, Mr Samuelson?'

Samuelson drew breath and sighed, obviously recalling some painful incidents in his past. 'I don't want to burden you with my past history, Mr Gould. It's enough to say that my family and I escaped from Amsterdam during the war. I was young, of course, but I can still remember the look of the brownshirts as they passed through the city. I was lucky to escape, but my parents were killed.'

'I'm sure you had dreadful experiences in the war, I'm very sorry for your loss, sir,' Gould said, dutifully conveying sympathy, while directing the man to the matter at hand. 'But could you return to the visit you had this morning.'

'That's the point. The man looked very like the Nazi troops who took my family away. I could sense the evil in this man.'

'And how old was he?'

'Anywhere from thirty to fifty, I would say. He seems to have a foreign accent.'

'And could you identify him if you saw him again?'

'I'm not sure,' Mr Samuelson said, looking like the frightened old man he was. 'It was all such a shock, and he may have been in disguise.'

Gould drew a breath. 'The war ended nearly fifty years ago, Mr Samuelson. How could this man have been involved in taking your parents away?'

95

'I know what you're thinking, but with my background, I can sense Nazis. This man may be related to those stormtroopers or he may not, but I know he was a Nazi.'

'And did you buy this diamond?'

'I certainly did not. He grew angry and walked out, but someone else will be sure to buy it. It was a very valuable jewel.'

Gould stood up. He was not sure how to take this matter forward. He was very tempted to give Samuelson a lecture on the penalties for wasting police time, but something about the old man's frightened expression made it impossible not to sympathise with him. Gould looked at the fear in the old man's eyes and reflected on his painful history.

'Thank you for reporting this, sir,' Gould said. 'You were right not to buy this diamond if you were uncertain about its history. But the Nazis were defeated in 1945. I can't ask my officers to look for them now. I understand you are upset, Mr Samuelson. Is there anyone I can call to keep you company?'

'No, Inspector. Thanks to the Nazis, I don't have a family,' Mr Samuelson said, his face conveying a lifetime of pain.

Gould stood up. 'You have my sympathies on your sad history, Mr Samuelson. But I will take my leave now, sir. Please make sure you keep your doors and windows secure. There seem to be some very valuable items here. Goodbye.' Gould left the workshop and heard bolts on the door being closed behind him.

Walking back to his car, Gould reflected he understood why the constable had asked him to follow up the query. He shook his head at the sadness of Mr Samuelson's situation, but wondered if the man's mind was wandering in his old age. There was no evidence that the diamond was stolen. Gould told himself he would have to mark the incident as not needing further investigation. He reminded himself that his next call was to the de Beers office close by, which seemed likely to be a more important visit.

CHAPTER 23

L ater that day, David Gould looked around at the luxurious entrance hall of the head office of De Beers in Carlton House Terrace. As a senior police officer in the City of London, he was used to ostentatious displays of wealth, but this office still took his breath away. While waiting to be seen, he studied an informative display stating how the company was the sole supplier of raw diamonds from its mines in Botswana, Canada, Namibia and South Africa. A few of its finished products were on display and Gould uttered an involuntary gasp both at the beauty of the jewellery and the prices that they sold for. He knew the mark-up between the raw diamonds found in one of the company's mines and the finished products must be huge.

'Detective Chief Inspector Gould?' a voice with a slight South African accent called.

Gould stood up and offered his hand to the expensively dressed elderly man in front of him. 'Mr Thompson?'

'Yes, I am Julian Thompson. Please follow me.' Thompson led Gould through carpeted corridors before entering a large meeting room. 'I see you were studying our display in the lobby. How much do you know about the diamond trade, Chief Inspector? Perhaps I can tell you a little about it.'

Gould was minded to explain he was a busy man and had not come to the De Beers office for a lecture. However, he had no wish to offend Thompson. 'Please bring me up to speed, sir,' he replied. 'I am always willing to learn about activities in the City.'

'Well, basically De Beers was established in the 1880s by Cecil Rhodes – a controversial figure, who ended up controlling all the diamond mines in South Africa. The company is now owned by the Oppenheimer family. To cut a long story short we are still the sole suppliers of raw diamonds to the trade. As you can see, our head office is here in London and we are an important part of the local diamond market.'

'I see,' Gould said, hoping that Thompson would soon explain why the company had asked to see a senior detective.

'As you can imagine, we keep a close eye on the diamonds that come on to the auction market here in London,' Mr Thompson continued. 'We manage supply to keep prices stable. However, in the last few days, we have noticed a sharp increase in the number of diamonds coming onto the market. This is bad news for us as it means we have to hold back some of our sales, which obviously affects our profits.'

'Surely, supply of diamonds must fluctuate,' Gould said. 'If some rich widow dies and the estate sells her diamonds, that will increase supply. Such things must happen all the time.'

'Of course, but lately there has been an unprecedented supply of diamonds onto the market, which makes us suspicious.'

'Suspicious of what?'

'There are only two ways diamonds can come onto the market without our knowledge,' Mr Thompson began. 'One is through brand new previously undiscovered mines …'

'And, since you keep informed about the supply of diamonds, I'm guessing you know that hasn't happened,' Gould finished Mr Thompson's sentence.

'Exactly, or else a supply of existing diamonds has suddenly been unearthed …'

'Which you suspect is happening recently,' Gould said.

'That's right. Sometimes, diamonds change hands when the previous owner dies, and the inheritor decides to sell them. We have not noticed any particularly large estates in recent months, which makes us suspect some criminal has got control of diamonds – probably by theft.'

'Interpol would have informed us of any major burglaries

involving diamonds – and I don't remember reading about any recently.'

'That's our understanding,' Mr Thompson said. 'The only explanation is that someone stole diamonds a long time ago and is only now selling them.'

'If the theft has never been reported, it looks as if they had been stolen from someone who wishes to keep the theft secret. Probably a criminal himself in some way.' Gould suddenly stopped. He had remembered the story Philippa had told him that her grandfather may have been murdered by a Nazi criminal or a descendant of such a person, to get hold of diamonds missing for fifty years. Suddenly, his visit to Mr Samuelson's establishment seemed likely to prove more important than it had seemed at the time.

'I see from your reaction that you have some suspicions, Chief Inspector,' Mr Thompson said, smiling for the first time in their meeting.

'Yes, but it may come to nothing. There have been a couple of incidents recently that indicate some suspicious characters may have come into possession of a large cache of diamonds and are trying to sell them here in London. Tell me, Mr Thompson, have you heard anything of diamonds missing in Corsica since the war?'

'Well, yes, everyone in the trade has heard rumours of missing diamonds that were stolen by the Nazis and disappeared – but that is all they are – rumours.'

'Possibly, they are more than rumours. Leave this with me, Mr Thompson. I suggest I investigate the issue further and come back to you if I find anything.'

'I should say De Beers will be offering a reward of £50,000 for anyone who provides information leading to arrest of whoever is trading these diamonds illegally,' Mr Thompson said, in the formal tone of someone reading a legal text.

'Thank you, sir,' Gould said. 'That might help us in our inquiries.'

CHAPTER 24

The next day, Gould sat at his desk and thought about his visits to De Beers and to Mr Samuelson. He cast his mind back to the conversation he had with Philippa at her grandfather's funeral, which he had almost forgotten until his visit to de Beer's. He wondered how to approach Philippa to discuss the old man's possible murder. Gould and Philippa had worked on many cases in the past. For around a year they had been lovers, but those days were long gone. Their relationship was now purely professional, and at the moment, they were seeing very little of each other, as they were in different departments. Gould decided a meeting between the two of them was necessary.

Gould called Philippa into his office. 'How are you recovering from the death of your grandfather? It must have been a terrible shock,' Gould asked her after exchanging pleasantries.

Philippa reflected for a moment. 'Yes, I'm getting on with my life as much as I can,' she said. 'Obviously, old men die all the time, but Grandad shouldn't have died like that. As I told you, the Met thinks it was suicide. The coroner agreed with them.'

'But you don't …' Gould prompted.

'No, he would never have killed himself. He was a brave man,' Philippa said. 'I've seen his medals. Everyone who knew him called him a hero. All his old colleagues thought the world of him.' Philippa paused. 'But why did you want to see me?'

'It's your grandfather I wanted to talk to you about,' Gould said.

'It's kind of you to take an interest, but I don't want to burden you with my family problems, gov,' Philippa said, feeling embarrassed by Gould's questions.

'No, it's not out of sympathy. Something has come up that makes me interested in the case. Your grandfather's name was Police Sergeant Bill Cottrell, is that right?' Philippa nodded. 'Last time we spoke, you said he had been worried by something that happened in the war. Can you tell me exactly what he said about it?'

'He said he had been captured by the Nazis in Corsica in 1943, just before the island was liberated. An SS man called Muller had forced my grandfather to transport diamonds that had been brought from North Africa onto a boat. The boat sank but Grandad managed to escape. Eventually he was repatriated when the Americans had liberated the island. He did not know what happened to Muller.'

'You said he seemed worried and was feeling guilty. From what you said, he does not seem to have done anything to be ashamed of. He acted under duress while he was a prisoner of war. Why should he have felt guilty?' Gould asked.

'Yes, I know,' Philippa replied with a sigh. She gazed at Gould and realised she would have to describe what Bill had told her, despite any possible embarrassment. 'The shameful part is he kept some of the diamonds and sold them after the war. Also, he did not tell anyone in authority where the boat went down. I am not sure if he had some mad idea of trying to find the rest of the diamonds or if he wanted to forget about it all. Either way he sold the diamonds he had taken on the black market. He was a fine police officer for thirty years after that, but I'm ashamed he didn't hand the diamonds in. It's not how you expect a future police officer to behave.'

'And after all these years, Bill said he was being threatened by someone ...' Gould prompted.

'Just before he died, he said he received a threatening visit from someone with a foreign accent, but I never saw the person. Very soon after he spoke to me, he was found dead. The local police say it could have been suicide. Or alternatively they think he broke his neck by accident. But I don't buy it. I'm sure someone murdered him. Perhaps this Muller character – or some relative of his – is still alive and killed him. Or perhaps some criminal gang either here or in Corsica found out about what happened in 1943 and tortured him to tell where the boat sank.'

Gould sighed. 'Thank you for being so frank about your grandfather, Philippa. I didn't want to upset you. I've just made a couple of worrying visits. It looks as if you might be right. First, an elderly merchant was frightened when someone tried to sell a large diamond, with no provenance. The merchant refused as he was suspicious but, no doubt, some other trader will have bought it. Then, according to a senior man at De Beers, someone seems to have found a new supply of diamonds and is selling them on the market here in London, driving down the price.

'Suppose this Muller man, or a descendant, or an accomplice, tortured your grandfather and extracted information from him about where the boat sank. Let's say Muller – or whoever – then commandeered an expedition to retrieve the jewels. If this person was successful, and found this wreck off the coast of Corsica, then he could have started selling them on the London market.'

'That would explain everything,' Philippa said, excitedly. 'I'm sure my grandfather was killed. He would never have committed suicide. He was telling the truth when he said he was being threatened.'

'It would make a complete and believable story, but we're detectives. We're supposed to find proof, not make up stories that seem believable.'

'Can I be assigned to this case, gov?' Philippa asked, her voice raised in enthusiasm. 'I'd do anything to find out who killed my grandfather.'

Gould paused. 'We don't endorse personal vendettas, you know, Philippa. We need to have impartial officers. I should appoint someone else to this case.'

'Oh, but, gov, I'd do anything to be involved. You know I'm a good detective. Can't you think again?' Philippa pleaded as, without thinking, she leant across to get closer to Gould.

Gould gazed at Philippa thoughtfully. He could tell how much Philippa wanted to work on this case, and revealed a decision that he had already made, though others might consider it unorthodox. 'Relax, Philippa you don't have to beg. I've asked the commissioner to put you on this case, and he's agreed. He said it might help us having someone connected with the original case on the team.'

Philippa smiled. 'Thank you, gov, I won't let you down. So, how do we take this forward?'

'The first step is to find out what really happened in Corsica in 1943, just before the Nazis left. We need to find out if your grandfather was remembering things from so long ago clearly or not. There is a unit in the British Army that is still trying to find treasures from the war,' Gould said. 'The commissioner has asked us to liaise with them. I have an appointment with a Colonel Davies at the Ministry of Defence tomorrow. Now you're on the case, I'd like you to come with me. I've told Davies what little I knew about your grandfather's story. He has been researching this area and is keen to meet Lieutenant Cottrell's granddaughter.'

CHAPTER 25

The next day, Gould and Philippa waited in the reception area of the Ministry of Defence main offices in Whitehall. They looked across at Horse Guards Parade, where two sentries in ceremonial uniform stood guard, as tourists took their photographs. Philippa's mind went back to school visits to London, and how much she used to enjoy seeing the sights. Suddenly, her mind returned to the present, as she was startled by an aristocratic sounding voice behind them.

'They're a splendid sight, aren't they? The only trouble is no one is sure what they are exactly guarding as people can walk though there quite freely.' A man in his mid-thirties in the uniform of an army colonel approached them. 'How do you do. I am Colonel Davies, and you must be DCI Gould and ...'

'Yes, I am DCI David Gould, and this is Detective Sergeant Philippa Cottrell,' Gould said.

'I'm pleased to meet you,' Philippa said as the three shook hands.

'So, Bill Cottrell was your grandfather,' Davies chatted to Philippa, as they walked along the corridor. 'His name is in our records.'

'Yes, that's right. I suppose I am here in a personal capacity as well as part of the team investigating his death. There is also large supply of suspicious diamonds that has suddenly appeared on the market,' Philippa said as they entered Davies' office and a junior member of staff brought the visitors refreshments.

'So, how much do you know about Rommel's treasure, Philippa?' Davies asked.

Philippa looked baffled. 'Nothing, really. I've heard of Rommel,

104

of course. He was a German general in the war, but I don't know about any treasure.' She reflected she appreciated Davies's enthusiasm for his area of expertise, but she was not sure where this conversation was heading.

Davies proudly showed Gould and Philippa a book entitled Rommel's Treasure. 'I wrote this book a few years ago, and it sold quite well,' Davies said. 'As you can see, this topic is a special interest of mine.'

Philippa felt uncomfortable that Davies was talking to her rather than David Gould. 'It sounds as if we have come to the right source,' she said, her voice conveying a need to be polite.

'Yes, it's wonderful for me to meet someone related so closely to one of the main participants. No historian knew about your grandfather's involvement until now,' Davies said.

'No, I had never heard of Rommel's treasure. I did not know about my grandfather's time in Corsica at all until quite recently,' Philippa said. She felt uncomfortable at the intense excitement her story seemed to have aroused in Davies.

'Well, let me summarise my book. Rommel was head of the Afrika Corps in North Africa,' Colonel Davies said, with the practised delivery of an experienced lecturer. 'All the military experts agree he was an excellent general. For a long time, he pushed the British and Commonwealth forces back, but when Montgomery took control, the Germans started to lose ground. Eventually, of course, they were kicked out of North Africa altogether, and carried on fighting in Europe. The British had a great respect for Rommel as a general and a man.' Davies's voice grew warmer, and it was obvious that he shared the general high opinion of Rommel. 'Eventually, Rommel fell out of favour with Hitler and was encouraged to commit suicide – a sad end to a brilliant career.'

'So why did Rommel have a treasure?' Philippa asked, after a pause.

'It's a bit of a misnomer, really. Rommel was relatively

105

honourable, but he had several members of his staff who took pleasure in stealing jewels from the local Jewish families in North Africa. The worst man was called Walter Rauff – he was a dedicated Nazi who was happy to take part in Hitler's campaign to exterminate the Jews in North Africa. For our purposes he was also happy to confiscate – steal, really – large amounts of valuables from the local Jewish population and almost anybody else.

'Once the Germans decided to evacuate North Africa, they obviously had to transport all these valuables across the Mediterranean Sea. They shipped it all to Corsica in the first instance, then when they were close to losing the island, the local troops were ordered to transport the jewels to Germany. Apparently, Hitler wanted to mount a big display to show off his wealth.'

'And what happened then?'

'That's where the story goes cold. The treasure never arrived in Germany, and lots of people think it sunk somewhere off the coast of Corsica, but it has never been recovered as far as we know.'

'As far as you know?' echoed Gould.

'Exactly,' Davies said, his voice rising in excitement. 'There have been many crooked people over the years who would have loved to get their hands on the treasure. The Corsican Mafia for one, but if they have found it, they have not told anyone. There have also been some more legitimate people looking for it – one rich man called Link in particular. Either it doesn't exist – or it does and has never been found. My own theory, for what it is worth, is that it is still out there – at the bottom of the sea.'

'So, what can you tell us about Bill Cottrell's war record, Colonel?' Gould asked.

'Well, everything you told me that Bill Cottrell told Philippa matches the known facts,' Davies said, opening up an ancient-looking paper file. 'He was a lieutenant involved in undercover work in Corsica in 1943. There is no doubt a large number of valuables were transported through Corsica after the Allies won in North Africa. It went missing around the time the Nazis lost the island to the Allies. There is a theory that it was due to be sent to Berlin to make a grand display for Hitler. Whatever happened, as far as we can see the gold and diamonds never arrived in Berlin.

'So, it could have sunk as a result of Allied gunfire hidden by a Nazi hoping to recover it once, as he hoped, Germany won the war. It could have been stolen by a Nazi, or Nazi supporter, hoping to sell it on the black market. Perhaps the Corsican Mafia found it and sold it, or …' Davies's voice tailed away.

'Or what, Colonel?' Philippa asked.

'I hate to speak ill of the dead, officers, but perhaps, as he said, the late Bill Cottrell hid then sold some of the diamonds. Perhaps he took more than he admitted. I'm sorry, Philippa, but that was theft, and the diamonds should even now be returned to their rightful owner – whoever that may be.'

'But I don't know what happened to any money Grandad obtained from selling the diamonds,' Philippa said, as tears came to her eyes.

'I propose we visit Corsica and see what the authorities there can tell us,' Gould said.

'Perhaps I should come with you to get your inquiry started, Chief Inspector,' Davies said. 'I know a good deal of the history of the case, and I could help with the military side.'

Gould stood up. 'That looks like a plan, Colonel.'

'Very good, but call me Christopher. Let's be on first name terms. We could fly to Corsica together.'

* * * *

After his visitors had left, Davies looked out of his office window and watched Gould and Philippa cross Whitehall and walk in the direction of their City of London headquarters. He admitted to himself he was intrigued by their visit. As a historian, he was used to working in an academic environment. To be part of a real-life criminal investigation was a new experience for him, and he was looking forward to it.

Colonel Davies was not sure what to make of David Gould and Philippa Cottrell. They were obviously two experienced detectives used to dealing with criminals. He realised most people regarded historians, such as himself, as ivory tower academics, who served no practical purpose. He feared that once these two detectives had obtained whatever information they felt was useful for the case, they would cast him aside.

To avoid this happening, Davies had decided to be less than fully open about his research. One particular nugget he wanted to keep up his sleeve was that Muller had been interrogated by the Russian army in 1945. Davies had only found about this in the files because he could read Russian. This interview had given useful information about where the yacht that Muller had commandeered had sunk. Most of the searches that had gone on since the war had focussed on a site several miles from the location that Muller had described in 1945.

Colonel Davies had often fantasised about using his knowledge to find Rommel's treasure for himself. He felt this would be a useful addition to his likely pension. He had kept an eye on Muller's movements over the years and had realised that, with the fall of the Iron Curtain, Muller was likely to make his move to find the cache in Corsica. Davies was able to use his contacts in military intelligence to flag up Muller's recent flight to Bastia. He had passed the information on to the local Corsican police, but did not know if anything had been done with this.

Davies had visited Bastia as part of his research some years before, and, now the diamonds had apparently been discovered, he felt another visit to Corsica was needed. Davies told himself that, all things considered, a trip to Corsica with the City of

London police, paid for by the army, to investigate his particular area of interest, was something he was looking forward to. He could carry on more research on his own, once he was on the island.

CHAPTER 26

A few days later, Gould, Davies and Philippa Cottrell arrived at the main police station in Bastia. They had enjoyed the flight from London and had spent part of the previous day becoming acquainted with the island. Gould had never visited Corsica before, and Davies and Philippa helped to bring him up to speed. Davies gave more information about Corsica during the war, based on his book.

After they passed the security checks, the three visitors were ushered into the office of Capitaine de Police Anton Dupree. He turned out to be a dark, stocky man in his forties, who explained he dealt with historical crime for Corsica. Although Davies spoke fluent French, Gould and Philippa were pleased that Dupree was willing to speak in English. However, he gave the impression that he regarded the visit from the British officials as a nuisance.

'This is my sergeant, Lucas Clement,' Dupree said, introducing his junior colleague. Clement looked to be in awe of Dupree, but less than interested in the British officials' visit. Clement had light hair, which from Gould's limited observation, was unusual in Corsica. As the two groups shook hands, Gould vaguely wondered about Clement's background. Gould immediately marked him down as an officer who would do as little as possible to get by.

'I've read the file that you sent me, of course, Chief Inspector Gould,' Dupree began, when everyone had sat down. 'But perhaps it will be easier if we assume I know nothing about the case. Please explain the purpose of your visit in your own words.'

'Of course,' Gould replied. 'First of all, thank you for agreeing to see us. My colleagues and I are investigating a sudden increase in the sale of diamonds in the City of London recently. It seems likely that these jewels may have been retrieved from a cache of diamonds lost in Corsica by the Nazis in 1943, when, as you know, they lost control of the island.'

'Yes, a date dear to all Corsicans,' Dupree interrupted. 'We were the first part of France to be liberated.'

'Indeed so,' Davies said. 'At that time, and ever since, there have been many rumours that jewels were lost near the island. Some people say they were on their way to Berlin for a large display of the valuables Hitler had stolen. Lots of research points to a yacht containing the jewels being sunk near Bastia. The wreck, if it exists, has never been found, and the jewels may still be at the bottom of the sea.'

'Everyone in Corsica has heard those rumours, Colonel,' Dupree said. 'There have been many expeditions to discover these valuables, but none have been successful. A rich American called Edwin Link is searching for the treasure, as we speak. People have been looking for it ever since the war. If the treasure existed, I'm sure it would have been discovered by now.'

'We feel the treasure certainly exists and we suspect it has recently been discovered,' Gould said. 'The difference is that we suspect these particular treasure hunters had expert information they extorted from Philippa's grandfather.'

Dupree turned to Philippa. 'Your grandfather? I don't understand, Sergeant Cottrell.'

'My grandfather was assigned to help the Corsican Resistance during the war. He was captured just before the Liberation. Before he died,' Philippa began, 'my grandfather told me he had been ordered to transport diamonds from Bastia when he was a prisoner of war here in 1943. He never told anyone about what happened then, but, a month ago, he had an uninvited visit from someone who threatened him. My grandfather told me he was worried and the same day he was found dead. I believe he was murdered by someone to reveal the location of the diamonds.'

Dupree spoke in a condescending tone. 'I am sorry for your loss, Sergeant, but your grandfather was presumably an old man. It is hardly surprising that he died. You think he was murdered. What do the local police think?'

Philippa looked embarrassed. 'They think he committed suicide or fell out of bed accidentally.'

'Presumably they viewed the body, and they are the experts,' Dupree said. 'Their opinions should be respected. Possibly your views are coloured by understandable loyalty to your grandfather. But, let us suppose you are right, do you have any clues as to who committed this alleged murder?'

'One clue was that the man in charge of the Bastia area in 1943 was a high-ranking Nazi called Felix Muller. He was the man who captured my grandfather and ordered him to transport diamonds by boat to Italy. However, the vessel sank close to Bastia. If Muller is still alive, he would be the prime suspect. The man who came to see my grandfather the first time was much younger, but he could be an associate or a relative of Muller. Then, there was a sighting of two men acting suspiciously around the time my grandfather died – one of them older, who could perhaps have been Muller.'

Dupree gave a theatrical sigh. 'I must say, at first sight, your case does not seem very convincing. An old man makes up a fantasy about transporting diamonds when he was a prisoner of war in 1943. A little later, according to your colleagues who are charged with investigating the case, he fell out of bed and died either as suicide or as an accident.'

Philippa raised her voice in anger. 'If you're not going to investigate the matter, we won't bother you any more.' She put her papers in her case and stood up, ready to leave.

Dupree gave a half-smile. 'Sit down, Sergeant Cottrell. I said at first sight your case was not convincing. However, the name of Muller is well known in Corsica. He was a household name – a household enemy, you might say. He was possibly the most hated man in Corsica at the time. Most people think he was lucky not to have been executed after the war for his crimes. Many people would be happy to kill Muller themselves. As a police officer it would be my duty to protect him from any attack but, as a patriotic Corsican, I might look the other way if people want to execute him with their bare hands.'

Gould sat up in surprise. 'Are you saying you know where Muller is? Is he still alive? Can we arrest him?'

'I know exactly where he is, but there is no hope of making an arrest,' Dupree said. 'For better or worse, Felix Muller is very dead. He is in our police morgue. He was killed by a harpoon. His body was found two weeks ago in Bastia harbour, so there is no hope of making him answer for his crimes.'

Gould yelled with surprise. 'That changes the case completely. Many people believed Muller had been killed in the war. Now, you say, he was killed two weeks ago. So he could have tortured and then killed Bill Cottrell two months ago. Do you know what he was doing before he was killed? Could he have been looking for the treasure he lost in 1943?'

'That could be possible,' Dupree said. 'Our force has just started our investigation. We will try to find who killed Muller, of course. But I must tell you, whoever it is they will be a hero to many Corsicans.'

'I must say,' Sergeant Clement intervened, 'we have not had much cooperation from the public when we have been trying to find the person who killed Muller.'

'All three of us would be happy to help you in your inquiry,' Gould said.

'We know that Muller was captured by the Russians at the end of the war,' Davies said. 'He spent two or three years in a Russian prisoner of war camp, but do you know what happened to him after that?'

'Muller was released into East Germany, as it was,' Dupree said. 'He seems to have continued his criminal activities in East Berlin.

There were a few convictions for theft, but nothing in the last few years. I don't know why Muller decided to return to Corsica earlier this year – he must have known there were still plenty of people here who would be more than happy to put a bullet in his heart.'

'So, you agree Muller must have had a good reason to return to Corsica where he knew he was hated,' Gould said. 'Let's say he realised that once the Berlin Wall fell, and he was free to travel, a trip to discover some of the stolen treasure would be worthwhile. He remembered the name of Bill Cottrell and discovered perhaps to his surprise that the diamonds and gold were still missing. The last person he knew to have seen them was Bill Cottrell. What's more natural, if you are a criminal, than to undertake a trip to London, torture Bill and obtain information on the best place to look for the diamonds?

'Assuming he was successful, perhaps he came back to Corsica and launched a boat with a crew to discover the diamonds. His plan was to sell the diamonds on the market somewhere himself. Then let's say his associates got greedy and killed him. Hence his body was found in Bastia harbour.'

Dupree looked sceptical. 'Or maybe some local with a grievance from the war decided to kill him for some unrelated reason.'

'Yes, but we know someone has the diamonds now,' Gould said. 'The selling has been going on since Muller was killed. The only real clue we have is a diamond trader in London who seems to think the seller had a foreign accent and was some kind of Nazi he had encountered in the past. He realised the seller was too young to have been in the war, but the poor man was terrified. Perhaps Muller had a son or some other relative who is selling the diamonds now. Either he killed Muller himself or he took the opportunity of Muller's murder to take over the business.'

'What do you think about David's theory of what happened, Capitaine?' Davies asked Dupree.

'It all hangs together as a – what's the English word – hypothesis, but that's all it is at the moment – an hypothesis,' Dupree replied, his tone conveying deep scepticism.

'You're right, of course,' Gould said. 'We have no proof yet. But it seems to fit all the known facts. Now is the time to do some proper police work and gather the evidence. Can we look at Muller's body?'

Dupree stood up. 'Yes, I am happy to cooperate with you, but I want to keep all options open. Tomorrow we'll go to the morgue and we must see if there is any evidence that Muller hired a boat to look for diamonds. If he had any sense, he would have gone in disguise to avoid any vigilante attack. Any crew he hired would be prime suspects if your hypothesis is true. It would be much easier if your diamond trader witness could identify the person trying to sell the diamonds.'

'I'm not too hopeful,' Gould said. 'The poor man seemed very frail and frightened out of his wits.'

CHAPTER 27

After the meeting, the three British visitors stood outside in the square outside the police station, discussing the meeting they had had with Dupree.

'The fact that Muller was killed so recently throws a whole new light on the case. It sounds very suspicious that he was murdered so soon after Bill Cottrell was,' Gould said.

'I agree. I can see you have a very active case, David,' Christopher Davies said.

'Yes, I think this is a police matter, now, Christopher,' Gould said. 'It's no longer purely a historical crime. I think Philippa and I can take this forward.'

Davies glared at Gould, obviously disappointed that his help was no longer needed. 'Well, I'll leave you to take the lead now. I think I've given you all the historical information I can. Feel free to get in touch with me any time.'

'Yes, that will be fine, Christopher,' Gould said. 'I think we can carry this forward ourselves now. I don't think we need to involve you anymore,' Gould added. He found it difficult to hide his eagerness to carry on the inquiry without the outside influence of Davies.

'Very well, I'll return to London. Come and see me if you think I can help with the rest of your inquiry,' Davies said, before shaking hands with the detectives and walking away.

Gould and Philippa stood outside the Bastia police station, deciding on their next steps. Philippa idly gazed up at the French tricolour flying high above the building, as Gould phoned for a taxi to their hotel. Just then a man in civilian clothes rushed up to them.

'DCI Gould, DS Cottrell, I'm so glad to have caught up with you,' he said. The two City of London police officers stopped to see what the man wanted. 'My name's Karl Jansen,' the man said, then stopped in surprise when he seemed to recognise Philippa.

'Karl, it's you, isn't it?' Philippa said. Turning to Gould, she added, 'Karl and I met when my grandad and I were on holiday here three months ago. It's a surprise to see you again.'

'I'm pleased to meet you. It's good to meet any friend of Philippa's, but I'm afraid we have nothing to say to members of the public,' Gould said, edging away from the other man.

'I'm not a member of the public. I'm sorry I misled you, Philippa. I only told you part of the truth. I'm a police researcher. I've been seconded from Interpol to the French federal police in Paris. I gather you've been to see Dupree.'

'You seem to know a lot about our business,' Gould said. 'We need to confirm your identity before we talk any more.'

Karl showed his Interpol warrant card. 'This seems to be in order,' Gould said, after examining it carefully. 'What can we do for you, Mr Jansen?'

'I wondered if we could discuss your investigation, Chief Inspector. There is a quiet bar on the next corner.'

Gould nodded assent. Once the three had received their drinks and looked around to make sure they were not being overheard, Gould turned to Karl. 'So how did you and Philippa meet, Mr Jansen?'

'I was having a meal at one of the hotels near here when you joined me, isn't that right, Philippa?'

'Yes, it was crowded, and we shared a table. We started chatting and Karl took me up to Calvi on the train. It was a great day out, wasn't it, Karl?'

'Yes, but then you flew back to London the next day and we lost touch. Your grandfather was with you on the trip, but I never saw him. I hope he's well.'

'No, he isn't,' Philippa replied, with tears in her eyes. 'He died in mysterious circumstances last month. I am sure he was murdered because of the time he spent in Corsica during the war.'

'Oh, I'm so sorry to hear that,' Karl replied, reaching out his arm to comfort Philippa. 'You must be devastated.'

'That is mainly why I am here. It looked as if whoever killed Grandad has got hold of Rommel's treasure and is selling diamonds on the London diamond market.'

Gould interrupted. 'Now, we have brought you up to speed with our investigation, Mr Jansen, perhaps we can return to the matter in hand. I must say you seem to have an unusual way of conducting official business. Why are we meeting in this bar, and not in police headquarters?'

'That's why I wanted to see you, Chief Inspector. I am the head of a team investigating the whereabouts of various treasures stolen by the Nazis during the war and have never been recovered. One of them is Rommel's treasure, which went missing in 1943. Your name came up on the Interpol confidential database. It highlights investigations of interest to us including your visit to Corsica. I decided to come to see if we could cooperate in some way. I wasn't expecting to see you, Philippa – that's a wonderful surprise.'

'It sounds as if we are all on the same side, Mr Jansen,' Gould replied. 'But I still don't understand why we are meeting here and not in Capitaine Dupree's office. He is investigating the death of Felix Muller, which I assume you know about. Why do we not all work together?'

'We were very interested to learn that Muller had been killed. The Corsican police are obviously in the lead in investigating Muller's murder, but they have not always been helpful to us in Interpol. You must understand the mafia is very strong in Corsica, DCI Gould,' Karl said, looking around to make sure they were not being overheard. 'Everyone knows they have tentacles everywhere and control some officers in the local police. To be honest, I don't think that Dupree can be trusted. His sergeant is called Clement – did you meet him?' Gould nodded. 'I also have suspicions about him.'

'Are you saying that Dupree or his sergeant is corrupt in some way? That is a serious allegation, Karl. Do you have any evidence?' Philippa asked.

'Tell me. Was Dupree enthusiastic about investigating the murder of Felix Muller?'

'He seemed sceptical about my involvement in the case,' Philippa said. 'Like most Corsicans, I imagine, he seemed pleased that Muller was murdered. He needed persuading to involve us in investigating the case, as he had some misgivings. Generally, it didn't seem suspicious to us. Did it to you, David?'

'Why don't we have a meeting with Dupree, Karl?' Gould asked. 'Then you could explain your worries to him.'

Karl slammed the table and startled some of the other customers at the café, who looked around curiously. 'No,' he said, 'it is essential that you do not tell Dupree about my interest in the case.'

'Why not?' Gould asked.

'Don't you see?' Karl said, looking from Gould to Philippa and back again. 'The mafia may well have killed Muller to get control of the diamonds. If Dupree is in the pay of the local mafia, he will have been told not to investigate this case properly. If the mafia know about me, my life would be in danger. It is essential that you don't tell Dupree anything about me.'

Gould gazed at Karl thoughtfully. 'It seems a shame that we can't cooperate. We should both be working to the same end. To be honest, I'm not sure which of you to trust, but it's not my job to come between the French police and Interpol. Leave me your contact details and I'll arrange to meet you when anything comes up. But until we know more, I agree we won't tell Dupree about your interest.'

* * * *

After leaving Gould and Philippa, Colonel Davies had decided to take a walk around Bastia. He was offended that the two City of London police officers so obviously felt they no longer needed his assistance. He told himself that he was well-respected as a leading expert on recent Corsican history and was sure he could have offered useful help.

Davies walked around Bastia harbour, mulling over his hurt pride. Suddenly, he noticed Edwin Link's huge yacht, which he recognised from press reports. He had read about Link's many expeditions to find Rommel's gold. Davies felt sure that the wealthy Texan would pay good money for information on the treasure for which he had been searching for so long. Davies walked up to the gangway and shouted that he wanted to see Mr Link.

After some discussion with people inside the yacht, the crewman allowed Davies to come on board. He was guided into Link's opulent office. Link stood up as he entered.

'Colonel Davies, is it?' Link said, coming forward, without offering to shake hands. 'You asked to see me, but I do not know how I can help the British Army.'

'It's more what I can do for you, Mr Link,' Davies started. 'I understand you are trying to find the gold the Nazis left behind somewhere near Corsica in 1943. I am something of an expert on the subject of Rommel's treasure. You may have seen my book on the subject.'

'Perhaps I have, but I do not understand,' Link said. 'Why should an officer in the British Army want to help me?'

'I am primarily a historian, Mr Link. If you were to pay me, I could undertake some historical research. I already know quite a lot of information that would be useful to you.'

'And what would your commanding officer say if he knew you were helping me?'

'He would be shocked,' Davies answered. 'That is why I propose that we keep this conversation secret. I'm sure we can reach an agreement that will benefit both of us.'

Link looked dubious, but then smiled. 'Help yourself to a drink, Colonel,' he said. 'You interest me hugely.'

CHAPTER 28

The next day, Dupree and Clement ushered Gould and Philippa into the autopsy room of Bastia police station. Clement opened a heavy door and showed them the naked body of an elderly man. Gould was familiar with the scent of death, but the smell, together with the heat of Corsica, made even him retch. Dupree introduced Gould and Philippa to the pathologist.

'This is Dr Delyon,' Dupree said. 'He undertook the autopsy on the body.' The two visitors shook hands with the pathologist.

'How do you do,' Gould said. 'We're interested in knowing how Felix Muller came to be killed. What can you tell us about the deceased, Doctor?'

'The body was of a man in his early seventies,' Dr Delyon said, reading from his notes. 'He was in good health for his age. He was found in the sea, but there was little water in his lungs, so he had not drowned. The cause of death was a sharp object piercing his heart. The police gave me a harpoon, which had some blood and hair of the deceased on it. That would be consistent with the observed injuries to the deceased.'

Philippa gazed at the dead man, with mixed feelings. She knew, more than most people, how much evil this man had done in the world in general and to her grandfather, both in the war and, more recently, when he was almost certainly one of the two men complicit in Bill's death. Muller looked like any other old man as he lay in the mortuary. She fought an urge to desecrate Muller's body in some way. She told herself that he would have to answer to God, if he exists, for his crimes. In any event, Muller was beyond any revenge she could offer. The only constructive action was to make sure the younger of the two thugs in her grandfather's nursing home was brought to court, and jailed for her grandfather's murder. She forced her attention to Gould's conversation with Dr Delyon.

'And do you have any doubts he was murdered?' Gould was asking.

'I can certainly visualise a malicious person shooting him with the harpoon and causing his death,' Delyon said. 'But accidents with harpoons happen frequently in the waters around Corsica every summer, so an accident is also quite possible. If I was a betting man, though, I would say it was most likely murder.' Delyon paused.

'Please continue, Doctor,' Gould prompted.

'I should warn you that it may be difficult to obtain a conviction for murder in this case. Once they learned the victim was a prominent member of the Nazi occupiers of the island during the war, a local jury would probably say it was an accident. Then buy the accused man a round of drinks,' Delyon added, with a half-smile.

'And how did the police identify the body as Muller's?' Gould asked.

'He had his German passport in his pocket,' Dupree replied.

'That's surprising,' Gould said. 'You'd think a man with a million enemies on Corsica would want to keep his identity secret.'

'It is odd, but it's true. I have his passport here,' Dupree said, taking a passport in a plastic wallet from a file. 'Perhaps he was too arrogant to hide his past.'

Gould studied the waterlogged document. 'Has anyone identified the body?'

Dupree shook his head. 'No, we normally look for a family member, but we haven't been able to find anyone who will admit to being Muller's relative.'

'I can't imagine Muller coming here for a holiday. As far as I can see, the only logical reason for him to come to Corsica would be to dig up some loot he left here when the Germans were kicked out in 1943,' Gould said.

'That remains to be proved, but I agree it seems a reasonable hypothesis,' Dupree said. 'The next step is solid police work. Your theory is that he was looking for treasure somewhere at sea. I will have our uniformed colleagues find out if Muller hired a yacht while he was here.'

'That would be very useful, Anton,' Gould said.

'We've found one interesting fact about Muller's time on the island.' Dupree said, opening an ancient-looking paper file. 'This is from 1944. It's a report on the follow up to the Liberation. It seems that Muller had a local mistress while he was in Corsica.'

'What do we know about her? Is she still alive?'

'Her name was Amelia Luri. She was given a hard time by her neighbours after the Liberation. The police found no evidence that she had done anything illegal, and she was not charged with any offence. The main thing is she is still alive and still at the same address.'

'We must see her,' Philippa said. 'My grandfather knew her. He visited her when we were on holiday here. He thought she may have betrayed him to Muller, but she denied it.'

'Yes, I have someone outside her house now,' Dupree said. 'She is at home, and I suggest we go around to see her right away.'

'We're ready now,' Gould said, then turned to Delyon. 'Thank you for your help, Doctor. You have been very helpful.'

CHAPTER 29

Two hours later, Gould and Cottrell stood to one side as Dupree knocked on the door of a small house in the mountainous area close to Corte. Philippa recognised it as the house she had taken her grandfather to visit. Amelia had not seen Philippa's face while she had been waiting in the car on her earlier visit, so there was no reason for Amelia to recognise Philippa. Eventually a woman in her seventies, that Philippa recognised as Amelia, opened the door.

'Que voulez-vous?' Amelia's unfriendly voice rang out.

'Madame Luri? I am Capitaine Dupree. I see from the file that you speak English. These are my colleagues from the City of London police. May we come in?'

'What file? Why should the police be interested in me? Is this about Felix? Can't you leave me alone after all these years?' Amelia said, looking around to make sure she was not being overheard.

'Please may we come in, Madame?' Dupree said. 'I'm sure you don't want your neighbours to hear what we have to say.'

'Very well, if you must,' Amelia said, standing to one side, to allow her visitors to come in.

'Please tell us about your relationship with Felix Muller, Madame Luri,' Dupree said, once they were all inside the house.

'What do you want to know?' Amelia said. 'As everyone seems to know, I slept with him during the war because I didn't want to go hungry. Does that seem wrong to you?'

'We are not here to judge you, madame,' Philippa said. She could see the hurt that had built up in this woman for the past fifty years.

Although Philippa's words were intended to be sympathetic, they seemed to infuriate Amelia. 'Judge me?' she shouted. 'I should think not. What can you young ones know what life was like back then?'

Philippa glared at Amelia. 'I believe you once knew my grandfather, Bill Cottrell, Madame Luri. He came to see you last summer. He was worried you may have betrayed him to the Nazis. Since you saw him, he has died.'

Amelia studied Philippa's face. 'Yes, I do remember Bill Cottrell. I was surprised when he came to see me. You look a bit like him. I am sorry for your loss, of course. He was a good man. He came to see me not long ago. He seemed to think I had betrayed him, but I never did. I told him it could have been his sergeant – I never trusted him. My heart was always with the Resistance, even if I slept with Felix so I would not starve. But why have you come to see me?'

'I believe my grandfather was killed, Madame Luri,' Philippa said. 'We believe he was killed by Felix Muller.'

'How could that be?' Amelia asked. 'I've always assumed Felix died long ago.' Her lies did not convince her visitors.

'If you say you never loved Herr Muller, this news should not be as painful as it might have been,' Dupree said. 'Felix Muller's body was found in Bastia harbour two weeks ago. It looks as if he was murdered.'

'Dead, my God,' Amelia said, staggering back in a convincing display of shock. 'How did he die?'

'He was killed by a harpoon in Bastia harbour,' Clement said. 'We suspect he was searching for missing gold and diamonds. So, you see we are not looking into ancient history from the war. Our investigation is very relevant to the here and now. Somebody killed Muller and is still walking around Corsica as a free man – or woman,' Dupree added with his eyes fixed on Amelia's face.

'Woman? Do you mean me?' Amelia asked, after a pause. 'Do you really think I killed Felix?'

'You tell us, madame,' Gould said. 'You would have a very strong motive to kill Muller. He left you without a second thought when he went back to Germany. You were left here to be lynched by the partisans. I've seen pictures of what they did to female collaborators once the Germans had left. It was not pretty. You must have hated the man who caused that to happen to you.'

'I have not seen Felix since he left Corsica in 1943. I had no idea he was on the island. I assumed he was dead or back in East Germany.'

'We understand Muller returned to Corsica two months ago,' Dupree said. 'Are you saying he did not come to see you?'

'Certainly not. He must have known that I would want to kill him.'

'And did you kill him, madame?' Gould asked.

'No, I did not,' Amelia said. 'I never saw him.'

'I believe you have a son, Paulu,' Dupree said. 'Is Muller his father?'

'He may have been,' Amelia answered, with a shrug.

'Do you know if Paulu has been in touch with Muller at all?'

'No, of course, he hasn't. He would have told me.'

'And is there anything else you can tell us to help track down Felix Muller's killer?' Dupree asked.

'No, nothing,' Amelia said.

'Very well,' Dupree said. 'We will leave you. Please phone us if anything occurs to you. I should say, lying to the police is a serious offence, Madame Luri.'

'I am well aware of that. One thing – what have the City of London police got to do with it?'

'As my colleague said, Muller is the prime suspect for the murder of William Cottrell in London a month ago,' Gould said. 'We suspect Muller found a large cache of diamonds from the war days. We believe the person who killed Muller took them and has started selling them in London. We would very much like to interview that person for two murders and theft of a large number of diamonds. I should say there is a large reward for the recovery of these diamonds.'

'I did hear rumours about Rommel's treasure,' Amelia said. 'I never believed it existed. Do you think it might have been true after all?'

'We think so, and Muller was trying to find it,' Dupree said, standing up. 'Please let us know if you think of any further information that would help us. Also please ask your son, Paulu, to come to Bastia police station and make a statement.'

Amelia ushered the visitors to the front door, with obvious relief. 'My son has nothing to do with this. Please leave right away.'

'Very well, madame,' Dupree said, as the four detectives left Amelia's house. They stopped for an exchange of views when they reached Dupree's car.

'Do you think she was telling the truth?' Gould asked.

'No, not at all,' Dupree said. 'She gave herself away with one of her answers. How did she know Muller was in East Berlin, if she had never been in touch with him?'

'Do we think she could have killed Muller?' Philippa asked.

'Somehow, I don't, but she had as strong a motive as anyone. We must keep her on our list of suspects,' Gould said. 'I would be interested to know more about this son of hers.'

'We will keep an eye out for Paulu Luri. We should find him soon,' Dupree said, preparing to drive away. After a while, he turned to Gould and Philippa. 'You must know that whenever there is murder and theft in Corsica,' Dupree said, 'the Mafia is usually involved in it. We know they have been trying to find Rommel's treasure for years. They wouldn't hesitate to kill Muller if they thought he had it. I'll arrange to interview the local chief – a man called Santoni – tomorrow. Let's see what he has to say. At the very least, we will show we suspect him. It should unsettle him. We can monitor his movements to see how he reacts.'

Gould and Philippa, remembering Karl's suspicion that Dupree could be in the pay of the Mafia, exchanged glances. 'We would be very interested in coming along to that interview, Anton,' Gould said.

* * * *

After the detectives had left, Paulu came from the bedroom, where he had been hiding. 'I was listening to all that,' he said. 'Why did you lie? The police will be sure to find out the truth. We both know Muller was here earlier this month. Someone may have seen him.'

'I wanted to give us some breathing space. They'll be sure to come back,' Amelia said. 'Now tell me what you have been up to with Felix.'

Paulu looked startled. 'How did you know about Felix and me?'

'I am not a fool, Paulu,' Amelia said. 'I've been down to Bastia and I saw you in the harbour with him. What were you doing?'

Paulu sighed. 'Yes, Muller asked me to help look for these diamonds that sank during the war. I crewed for him and some character called Walter, but one day they never came back. I wasn't sure what to do. At the end of the day, I returned the yacht to its owner and gave up. It was a dead loss – Muller and Walter never paid me the money I was promised. All I earned was the return of the deposit on the yacht. If Muller did find diamonds, it's the first I've heard of it. I don't have any.'

'You'd better think of some better explanation than that when those policemen return,' Amelia said. 'Felix may be dead, but they are still looking for some accomplice of his for double murder and theft of loads of diamonds.' She paused. 'And you are one of Muller's accomplices – like it or not. They think loads of diamonds are missing. If the police don't catch you, the Mafia will.'

Paulu looked scared. 'I think I'd better make myself disappear for a while,' he said. He grabbed his jacket and ran out of the house.

CHAPTER 30

The next day, Dupree called Gould to the harbour in Bastia. A frightened looking man was standing in front of him, next to Clement.

'This person says he hired his yacht about a month ago to a German called Schmidt,' Clement said. 'He didn't ask for any ID. A different man returned the yacht undamaged a week later and was given his deposit back.'

'Does he recognise this Schmidt from Muller's passport photo?'

'He thinks he does but isn't sure.'

'Did Schmidt say what the purpose of hiring the yacht was?'

'No.'

'Did he have any crew with him? A yacht of that size would need crew.'

'I didn't see any,' the man said, after translation.

'Did he leave the yacht in good condition? Was there any blood on it?'

'It was in good condition. I didn't see any blood,' the yacht-owner said, sulkily. 'I know who returned the yacht, though.'

'Who?' Clement asked.

'Paulu Luri,' the man said. 'I'm sure it was him.' The detectives exchanged glances.

'That's very interesting,' Gould said. 'It seems that Amelia has been lying to us. Can your scene of crime officers examine the yacht? There might be fingerprints or other traces. We need to find any crew Muller may have had.'

'Yes, they would be suspects for Muller's murder,' Dupree said. 'If so, they could be selling the diamonds in London. I suggest you leave that with us, David.'

'Isn't there any way we could help, Anton?'

'I think we have the expertise to deal with the inquiry here in Corsica. I suggest you find out more on the German side. It will be useful to find out more about Muller's career and family since the war. All we know is that he was a petty criminal, which doesn't tell us much. He must have accomplices, a wife or girlfriend or even children, back in Berlin, who would at the least be valuable witnesses.'

Gould thought for a while then nodded. 'Very well, Anton. Philippa or I will go to the old East Germany and see what we can find there. Then we'll compare notes, but, at the moment, I am sure Muller killed Bill Cottrell and found these diamonds. Then whoever murdered Muller is flooding the London market with them.'

Dupree nodded. 'As an individual, I believe you, David. But, as you know, as police officers, we deal with evidence and we don't have enough yet to make a case against anybody. Our forensic people will examine the yacht over the next few days. We will see what the evidence shows.'

* * * *

That evening, Gould and Philippa kept Karl up to date with developments over a meal in the same restaurant they had met in before. 'As you say, it looks as if Muller was killed as soon as he found the missing diamonds,' Karl said. 'It could be one of his crew, or perhaps someone else was watching Muller and killed him as soon as they saw he had found the treasure.'

'Who are the main suspects, do you think?' Gould asked.

'There are lots of them. Many people have wanted to find Rommel's treasure over the years. The mafia are one bunch – also a man called Edwin Link has been searching for the diamonds every summer for many years. You remember I pointed his huge yacht to you when we met before, Philippa. Link was in Bastia when Muller found the treasure and was killed. Link could be one possible suspect – quite a strong one, too, I think.'

'What do we know about Link?' Philippa asked.

'He was involved in aviation earlier on in his career, then invented the first machine to train pilots. It was called the Link trainer and was so successful he has not had to work ever since. He is very rich and can indulge his hobbies – one of them is looking for Rommel's treasure every summer.'

'Very nice for him, but it does not make him a murderer,' Gould said. 'It sounds as if he does not have the same financial motive as most people would.'

'But imagine he found out that he had been looking in the wrong place all this time. And what's more, the original Nazi thief had his hands on it. Could that make Link kill Muller? It sounds convincing to me,' Karl said. 'With his money, he could pay someone to kill Muller, while he has an alibi.'

'We'll bear Edwin Link in mind. What about the Corsican Mafia?' Gould asked.

'Yes, they must always be suspects. Santoni is the main local chief. I suggest we investigate him.'

'Dupree is arranging a meeting with him,' Philippa said.

Karl looked stunned. 'Really? Dupree is meeting Santoni? You must bear in mind what I told you about Anton Dupree. Interpol have grave doubts about him. He may be too close to the Mafia altogether,' Karl said.

'We'll bear it in mind, Karl,' Gould said, as the three police officers finished their meal. 'We'll see how he deals with Santoni when we meet him tomorrow.'

'I'd still love to know who betrayed my grandfather in 1943,' Philippa said.

'Does it matter now?' Karl asked. 'It was so long ago.'

'I think it does matter,' Philippa said. 'Could Amelia have given him away to Muller? Grandad assumed it was her but seemed convinced when she denied it. She told him it was his old sergeant.'

'Who is presumably either dead or peacefully retired back in England,' Gould said. 'It's hard to believe he could have killed Muller here in Corsica.'

'Santoni was around then. The Corsican Mafia were happy to collaborate with the Nazis when it suited them,' Karl said. 'They always claimed their motive was a free Corsica, but in reality, they were criminals who were only interested in money. That hasn't changed today. Be careful when you meet Santoni.'

Gould gazed thoughtfully at Philippa and Karl. 'All we have done so far is increase the number of suspects. We must start narrowing the field before very long.'

CHAPTER 31

The next day, Clement drove Dupree, Gould and Philippa Cottrell to Corte in the centre of Corsica. An unmarked police car followed them for additional security. The four police officers stood outside a villa, which seemed to be one of the largest and most luxurious on the island. The views from the entrance were stunning – the Mediterranean could be seen on the horizon behind a landscape full of vineyards.

'The bad guys always have the best properties,' Gould said.

'That seems to be true everywhere in the world,' Clement said, as the others nodded rueful agreement.

'Do you think this man Santoni might be the kingpin we are looking for?' Gould asked.

'Santoni certainly fits the bill,' Dupree said. 'He has the resources to finance Muller's expedition and wouldn't hesitate to kill him afterwards. We know he has killed before, but never been charged. As always, with men like Santoni, we need plenty of evidence before we can charge him with anything. He has several crooked lawyers ready to spring him if we have any weakness in our evidence.'

'How do we get the proof we need?' Philippa asked.

'It'll be very difficult. That's why I propose we interview him at this early stage,' Dupree said. 'I know he will be very charming and tell us nothing, but our visit might unsettle him. It will be interesting to see how he reacts. If you're ready, let's go.'

Dupree and Clement led Gould and Philippa up to the front door of the villa.

'We have an appointment to see M. Santoni,' Dupree said. The maid who answered looked terrified. Suddenly a voice came from behind the door.

'Let them in, Florence. I have nothing to hide from the police.' A dark well-dressed man aged about seventy came to the entrance. Philippa immediately recognised him as the passenger in the limousine that had driven too fast on her previous visit. 'Ah, Capitaine Dupree, always a pleasure. Won't you introduce me to your colleagues? I believe I recognise Sergeant Clement, but not the others.'

Clement spoke some words in Corsican to Santoni, who replied in the same language.

'We won't use that language, thank you, Sergeant,' Dupree said. Gould could tell Dupree's relationship with Clement was strained. 'M. Santoni, this is Detective Chief Inspector Gould and Detective Sergeant Cottrell of the City of London police,' Dupree said. 'Perhaps we can continue in English?'

'Of course – but to what do I owe the honour of this high-level visit?' Santoni asked.

'We are investigating the death of a man who is notorious in Corsica,' Dupree said. 'You will have heard of him – Felix Muller.'

'Muller – the Beast of Bastia. Is he dead?'

'Yes, he is. He was found dead in Bastia harbour two weeks ago.'

'I assumed Muller had died during the war. But what is he to me?' Santoni asked. 'And why are your British colleagues here?'

'I am here because a large number of illicit diamonds have turned up on the London market,' Gould said. 'And it looks very much that Muller was looking for some of the diamonds that he is supposed to have hidden before he left Corsica in 1943. We believe he found them recently. We suspect some unknown person then killed Muller soon after these diamonds were found. That person is now selling them on the market.'

'Very interesting, I'm sure. But I repeat what is this to do with me?' Santoni asked, leaning back in his chair.

'We all know you are behind most of the crime in Bastia. Probably you committed these crimes. If not, we thought you

135

might be interested if someone is setting up as a rival to you. Or, as an honest citizen, you could provide information to help us sort these crimes,' Dupree added, his voice dripping with sarcasm.

'Also, there is a large reward for further information about these diamonds,' Gould said. 'Some very big companies in London are worried about what is going on and are willing to pay large sums of money for information on the source of the diamonds.'

'That is interesting, thank you, Inspector. If that is all, I suggest we end this meeting. You have not mentioned any evidence linking me to this case. Despite what you have just heard, I am an honest businessman,' Santoni said with a chilling smile. 'As you may know, I have never been convicted of any crimes. Of course, I will be sure to tell you of any information that comes my way.'

'That will be very useful,' Dupree said.

'Well, perhaps we can call it a day there, lady and gentlemen,' Santoni said, standing up. Everyone knew the meeting was at an end. Santoni's superficial politeness had not fooled anyone there. Gould and Philippa instinctively knew Santoni would be happy to kill anyone who crossed him without a moment's hesitation – including Felix Muller, if he had anything that Santoni wanted.

* * * *

'Did we gain much from that visit, Anton?' Gould asked, as the four police officers climbed into Dupree's car outside Santoni's villa. 'I'm worried all we did was to alert a known criminal to our inquiries.'

'It's too early to say,' Dupree said. 'As I see it, there are two options. Let's say Santoni was involved in finding these diamonds and killing Muller. In that case, at least our visit shows the police are onto him and he should start to worry.

'Alternatively, Santoni hasn't been involved so far, and our visit was the first time he has known about Muller's presence in

Corsica. In that case, Santoni will want to know what has been going on in what he considers his area of control.'

'Which of those options do you believe, Anton?' Philippa asked.

'We always knew Santoni would deny involvement in any event. He is like a brilliant poker player, so he was not going to reveal if he was surprised by what we told him, or not. If you ask my guess, the news about Muller's murder was a surprise and he's going to want to find out what has been going on. I've arranged for a major surveillance exercise on Santoni and his associates. My colleagues will stay out of sight here and keep an eye on developments. If I'm right, there should be quite a lot of traffic of people being summoned to speak to the great man. I suspect he is going to send some of his henchmen out to find more about what's been going on with Rommel's treasure and Muller's murder.'

'What if you are wrong and Santoni is behind Muller's treasure hunting?' Gould asked.

'Then I guess he'll be wondering what or who put us in the police on to him. He'll want to find out if anyone in his organisation has been leaking information. In either case, I expect some moves from the Santoni gang. I suggest we leave my more junior colleagues to follow Santoni and his henchmen for the next few days.' Dupree paused, then added. 'One thing is certain. I would not want to be in Paulu Luri's shoes when the Mafia find him. Let's hope for his sake we find him first.'

'Good luck with finding Luri,' Gould said. 'If you drop Philippa and me in Bastia, we have some investigations of our own to carry out.'

CHAPTER 32

'Karl's involvement throws a spanner in the works,' Gould said to Philippa in their hotel restaurant that night. 'We have two forces – the French police and Interpol – who don't trust each other. Then we have Santoni from the mafia. Obviously, we can't trust the mafia, but somehow, I feel Santoni was telling the truth when he denied knowing about Muller's death.'

'And how do we know if Dupree or Karl are crooked or not?' Philippa asked.

'As far as we know, Anton Dupree is an honest cop. We have no evidence that he is bent. He needed persuading to follow up the mafia angle. But perhaps he was right to be sceptical. We only have Karl's word that Dupree may be corrupt.'

'How about Sergeant Clement? He has not said much so far. Perhaps he is reporting everything back to Santoni. I'd love to know what the two of them were saying in Corsican in that villa – they seemed too close for comfort.'

'The same applies to Clement. We have to assume he is an honest cop. There's no law against speaking Corsican. On the other hand, we don't know how far Karl can be trusted. I've checked with the Paris office of Interpol and Karl's story hangs together. His boss says he is following up on possible implications of Muller's murder. So, we know Karl is who he claims to be. I propose we'll keep the two strings of the investigation – with Dupree and Karl – separate.

'You liaise with Karl and I'll continue to meet with Dupree. I want to know who Muller could have met up with in Corsica. Did he have any comrades or some woman, apart from Amelia Luri, he could have decided to see again? I've agreed with Dupree that we'll follow up Muller's life in Germany.

'Why don't you go to Berlin with Karl and see what we can find about Muller's back history? Karl probably speaks German and can help while you are there. We don't want to tell Dupree about Karl though.'

Philippa nodded. 'Yes, gov. Next stop Berlin.'

CHAPTER 33

Two days later, Philippa and Karl stepped off the plane at Tempelhof – the old East German airport, which was struggling to find a market following the fall of the Berlin Wall. They had arranged to meet Polizeihauptkommissar Hans Schulz. Once they had passed through passport control a man in an ill-fitting suit approached them. His expression was not welcoming.

'Fräulein Cottrell, I am Hans Schulz. I have been ordered to welcome you.'

'How do you do? I am Detective Sergeant Philippa Cottrell. This is Karl Jansen of Interpol. May I call you Hans?'

Schulz replied after a pause. 'Perhaps that will be easier. Please come with me.'

The car journey through East Berlin showed the streets had changed little from the days of Communist control. It was still like entering a different country, far poorer than the old West Germany, which Philippa had visited in previous investigations. Schulz sat next to the driver in unfriendly silence.

'Has your job changed much since the collapse of East Germany, Hans?' Philippa asked, in an attempt to lighten the atmosphere.

'Yes, I am afraid it has. I expect it to change more in the future unfortunately.'

Once they had arrived at the police station, Schulz turned to the two visiting detectives. 'I should say that unlike most people here I am still loyal to the German Democratic Republic. I have been ordered to cooperate with you, but I don't have to like it. I haven't forgotten that bombing by the RAF killed many members of my family,' Schulz's voice was raised in indignation.

'I don't want to trade war stories, Hans,' Philippa said. 'I am here to trace what a convicted criminal called Felix Muller has been doing since the end of the war and when he was found dead in Corsica last month.'

Schulz looked through his papers, obviously trying to calm himself down. 'Felix Muller has been a small-scale criminal for most of the past fifty years. He has a criminal record, as long as your arm – I think that is the English expression. He has spent time in jail, mostly for smuggling. He hardly seems important enough to merit the City of London police being involved,' Schulz added, his voice dripping with sarcasm.

'Do you know why he suddenly decided to visit Corsica?' Karl asked.

'Apparently, he often talked to his cellmates about his time on the island. Perhaps he wanted to retire there?' Schulz suggested, with a shrug.

'Did Muller have any friends or associates here in East Berlin?' Philippa asked, struggling to keep her temper when faced with the unhelpful Schulz.

'I could not find any surviving family members. He does not seem ever to have been married. The only contact we could find was a young girlfriend called Zoe,' Schulz said. 'She works in a bar in the red-light district here. She should be there tonight.'

'Let's go there,' Karl said.

* * * *

That evening, Philippa, Karl and Schulz walked into the darkness of the Blue Angel club. There were pictures of scantily clad women on the walls and the carpets were threadbare. Philippa instinctively knew the only women who entered this place were the hostesses. The few male customers there gave her appraising glances, which she pretended to ignore.

Schulz flashed his warrant card to the unhelpful doorman and demanded to see Zoe. The doorman indicated for the three visitors to take a seat. Eventually he brought a pale blonde girl forward and indicated for her to speak to the visitors. She looked suspiciously at them.

'Zoe? Zoe Vogel?' Schulz asked

'Ja. Was wassen Sie?' she replied sulkily.

'Can you speak English?' Schulz asked, as Zoe nodded. 'I am Polizeihauptkommissar Schulz. My colleague from London has some questions for you.'

'Yes, hello, Zoe. I am Detective Sergeant Philippa Cottrell of the City of London police. This is Karl Jansen of Interpol. We would like to ask you about Felix Muller. I understand he was a friend of yours.'

'Last I heard, the City of London police don't have any powers in Berlin,' Zoe said. 'What if I refuse to talk to you?'

'Then I have a large number of questions for you and your boss,' Schulz said. 'I recognise the manager over there. I could close this bar down for a week while we investigate underage drinking and prostitution. Do you think he would like that? So, let's keep this friendly, shall we? Just answer Sergeant Cottrell's questions, and everything will be fine.'

Zoe glared at Philippa. 'Ask away, Sergeant.'

'I understand you had a relationship with Felix Muller. Please tell us about it. Were you close?'

'Yes, we were,' Zoe replied, nodding. 'We lived together for several years. Then a few months ago he left. He didn't even say goodbye.'

'Only, you must agree it seems a huge age gap,' Karl said. 'He was over seventy and I would expect a girl like you to go out with someone closer to her own age. Somehow, I guess that Muller must have had plenty of money to attract a girl like you. Do you know how he earned it?'

'Buying and selling things.' For some reason, Zoe seemed to Philippa to be scared of Karl.

'You mean smuggling.'

142

'In this career, I have learnt not to ask too many questions,' Zoe said.

'Do you have any idea where Muller went after he left you?'

'No, I told you. He just left me.'

'Did he ever mention Corsica to you?' Karl asked.

'No, where is it?'

'It's an island in the Mediterranean. He was there in the war. We believe he went there to recover some gold and diamonds he had hidden there.'

'Why don't you ask him?'

'Felix Muller was found murdered in Corsica a month ago,' Karl said, keeping his eyes fixed on Zoe's face.

'Murdered? The poor man! I know Felix did things wrong, but he didn't deserve that,' Zoe said, with tears in her eyes. Her surprise and distress seemed convincing.

'We would like to know who he associated with while he was in Berlin.'

'I was his only friend – if he had one, that is,' Zoe said. 'He used to go out to meet business contacts, but I never went with him. We both kept our work lives separate.'

Philippa made a quick decision. 'We need someone to identify Felix Muller's body in Corsica. He seems not to have any next of kin. We would like to fly you out there to confirm it is Muller.'

Zoe looked startled. 'Are you allowed to do that? Am I under arrest?'

'No, you are just helping us,' Philippa replied. 'Isn't that right, Hans?'

Schulz nodded. 'Yes, that's right. A trip to the Mediterranean sounds great to me – better than one of my cells, anyway, which is where you will be, if the Corsican police extradite you.'

'I can't afford to go there,' Zoe said, sullenly.

Philippa turned to Schulz. 'Can you make sure Zoe's boss pays her salary while she is away?'

'Of course,' Schulz said. 'If he doesn't, I am sure there are many offences we can ask the mayor's office to investigate.'

'You want me to fly to Bastia?' Zoe asked.

'Bastia. Yes, that's right,' Philippa said.

'I'm fascinated,' Karl intervened. 'How did you know the name of the town Muller was killed in? A moment ago, you didn't know where Corsica was.'

Zoe looked flustered. 'Perhaps Felix mentioned it once or twice. I didn't really know where it was or what it meant.'

'We will be returning there tomorrow,' Philippa said. 'I will book a ticket for you as well. I expect to see you at Tempelhof at this time,' Philippa said, writing down some details on her business card. 'Herr Schulz can make life difficult for you if you don't turn up.'

Zoe nodded her understanding and took the card in her hand.

144

CHAPTER 34

As they returned to their hotel, Karl turned to Philippa. 'What are you doing tonight?' he asked.

'Writing a report, I expect. David Gould is a tough taskmaster. He will want to know what I've been up to.'

'Why don't you let me show you the local sights? We could look at the shops on the Kurfürstendamm, then have dinner. There are some great restaurants there. We could have a wonderful evening.'

Philippa looked at Karl cautiously. 'Let's keep this strictly business, shall we? I can make my own entertainment, and I haven't made my mind up about you yet.'

'I understand. It'll be purely business,' Karl said, as Philippa nodded her agreement.

Later that evening, after seeing some of the sights of Berlin, Philippa looked across the restaurant table at Karl and smiled at him. She began to wonder if she wanted to develop any personal relationship with him. She had been feeling depressed since the death of her grandfather, and she told herself a fling with a good-looking and charming man like Karl was appealing.

Then she asked herself what she knew about him. She knew David Gould had checked Karl's credentials with his superiors at Interpol, and he was what he claimed to be. She did not want to turn into a suspicious woman with no private life. She told herself that, in any event, she was keen to support anyone who might help bring her grandfather's killers to justice. Karl seemed the person best placed to do that.

Philippa reached out and touched Karl's arm. 'Karl, do you think Muller killed my grandfather?'

'Yes, I am sure Muller or one of his associates tortured him to find information about Rommel's treasure. Whether your grandfather revealed what he knew – assuming he knew anything – I don't know. The fact that David Gould says there is a load of diamonds flooding the market suggests he did. Tell me, what sort of man was your grandfather?'

'I don't know now,' Philippa replied, thoughtfully. 'I always looked up to him. It was because of him I joined the police. I didn't know he was ever in Corsica until recently. It looks as if he did wrong by keeping then selling those diamonds. I still love him of course, but I can't help feeling disappointed in him. But the good he did in the police outweighed any bad he did when he was young. He didn't deserve to die like that.'

'Of course not,' Karl said, reaching out to comfort Philippa. 'We must try to find out who killed him.'

CHAPTER 35

While Karl and Philippa were in Berlin, significant progress was made in the case. Gould was talking to Dupree in Bastia police station when Clement came in.

'Pardon, gentlemen, but we have found Paulu Luri,' he said. 'He was acting suspiciously along the harbour.'

'Great,' Dupree said. 'Bring him in for questioning.'

An hour later, Paulu was sitting sulkily opposite Dupree, Clement and Gould.

'Tell me what you know about the murder of Felix Muller a month ago, M. Luri,' Dupree began.

'I don't know anything about it,' Paulu said, with his arms crossed.

Dupree sighed. 'The owner had a good look at the person who returned the yacht Muller had hired. The description he gave matches you closely, and he was sure it was you. Shall we get him here to identify you?'

'Oh, OK, it was me, I returned the yacht, but I didn't kill Muller.'

'Tell us the story from the beginning,' Gould said. 'How did you come to meet Felix Muller?'

'He visited my mother. He said he wanted someone to crew a yacht while he looked for diamonds. It sounded a good opportunity to make money.'

'Was Felix Muller your father?'

Paulu looked upset for the first time. 'Possibly. I asked my mother and she said she didn't know, but thought he was.'

'Carry on with your story, M. Luri,' Dupree said, his voice full of scepticism.

147

Paulu turned to Gould sensing he was the more sympathetic interrogator. 'Muller hired me to crew for him. He had a character called Walter with him. When we sailed back one day, they suddenly disappeared. They left without paying me. I just returned the yacht to the owner and left. I don't know about Felix Muller being killed.'

'Tell us about this Walter.'

'He worked with Muller. Walter would do the actual diving while Muller told him where to dive. I guess if Muller is dead, Walter may be the one responsible.'

'Would you recognise this Walter again?'

'Perhaps, he had a slight foreign accent. He was in his late thirties and had fair hair, but that might have been a wig.'

Dupree gave a very Gallic sound of disbelief. 'I don't believe a word you've told us, M. Luri. So, you're saying you never saw Muller being killed and know nothing about any diamonds.'

'That's right. You've got to believe me.'

'We don't believe you. We are going to re-enact the scene of Muller's murder and I am sure we will have plenty of witnesses coming forward. If you are guilty, admit it now. Killing Felix Muller would make you a hero to many people in Corsica.'

'But I didn't kill Felix Muller,' Paulu said, his eyes appealing for the detectives to believe him.

Dupree stood up. 'We have further enquiries to make. We will want you here to help with the re-enactment of the murder scene. You can go now but don't leave town, will you?'

'Yes, thank you, gentlemen,' Paulu said and left without bothering to hide his relief.

After Paulu had gone, Gould turned to Dupree. 'Why are you letting him off, so easily, Anton?' he asked. 'That man is a prime suspect.'

'Don't worry, David,' Dupree said. 'We will keep an eye on him. Sergeant,' he said, turning to Clement. 'Make sure we follow him – put several detectives onto the case. I've got a plan to hold a re-enactment of the murder, and we'll make sure Paulu Luri takes part, whether he wants to or not. Somehow, I guess that once he knows Santoni is looking for him, he'll suddenly decide the police are his best friends after all.'

CHAPTER 36

Gould arranged to meet Philippa and Karl as soon as they returned from Germany. 'So, what did you learn in Berlin?' he asked.

Karl answered, 'Only that Muller was a petty criminal for the forty-six years since he left the Russian prisoner of war camp. Soon after the Berlin Wall fell, he disappeared from his usual haunts. Soon afterwards, he turned up in Corsica. I can imagine him waiting for forty years for the chance to get hold of all the money he had control of in the war. He didn't seem to have any wife or family in Germany.'

'The only real contact was a girl called Zoe Vogel,' Philippa said. 'She's some sort of hostess in a seedy bar over there. She was living with him, but he disappeared suddenly, without saying goodbye. She says she's never been to Corsica, but she's probably lying. I arranged for her to fly with us here to identify Muller's body.'

'Let's do that, then we'll interview her with Dupree tomorrow,' Gould said.

* * * *

The next day, Gould and Philippa met Dupree in Bastia police station. Philippa told Dupree about what she had found out in East Berlin, without mentioning Karl's involvement. Dupree was very interested to hear about Zoe.

'So, what do you think? Could this Zoe be a murderer? Could this be a crime of passion? If Zoe is upset that he ditched her, could she have killed him?' Dupree asked.

'Some sort of crime of passion is always possible. But that wouldn't fit with these diamonds appearing for sale in London,'

Gould said. 'From what Philippa says, I can't see Zoe killing Muller, but possibly she could be being paid by someone or other for information about him. If so, it would be interesting to see who she's been seen with recently.'

'If she is involved and if she is seen with us, her life could be in danger,' Dupree replied. 'Let's bring her in for the identification first and then we have a few questions to ask her.'

* * * *

A few hours later, Gould and Philippa waited outside the autopsy room to await the results of Zoe's viewing of the body. She came out looking frightened, accompanied by Dupree and Clement.

'Thank you for helping us, Mademoiselle Vogel,' Dupree said. 'Can you confirm for the record that the man whose body we showed you is Felix Muller?'

Zoe nodded. 'Yes, that was Felix. It was horrible what someone has done to him,' she said, shivering. 'He didn't deserve to die like that.'

'Thank you for your identification. Now please accompany us to our interview room. My English colleagues and I have some questions to ask you.'

After Zoe and the four detectives had sat down in the interview room, Dupree started the questioning.

'I believe that, when you were interviewed in Berlin, you told Detective Sergeant Cottrell that you did not know where Corsica is and had never been here before. I put it to you that is a lie. Especially as later you admitted you knew Muller had been killed here in Bastia.'

Zoe looked at Gould, Dupree and Philippa. After a moment's thought, she seemed to decide to tell the truth. 'Oh, very well. I have been here before. I did follow Felix here. I was annoyed that he left me in Berlin without saying anything. He had mentioned Bastia a few times as somewhere that was important to him, so I followed him here. After I arrived, I read a lot about Rommel's treasure and thought that Felix might be involved. I saw him walking along the harbour here and confronted him. He wasn't pleased to see me and told me to go back to Berlin.'

'How did you feel about that?' Gould asked.

'I was angry, but I flew back to Berlin the next day and decided to forget about Felix. I never knew he had been killed until your colleagues told me the other day in Berlin.'

'We believe Muller was killed on 30 May. Were you here in Corsica then?'

'I don't know, I may have been,' Zoe replied, sulkily.

'We've checked and you flew back to Berlin on 31 May. That means you had the opportunity to kill Muller and then catch the next morning's flight,' Dupree said.

'I didn't kill Felix. I could never do anything like that.'

'I have your criminal record here,' Dupree said, standing up. 'There are many serious crimes shown. I believe you had the motive, means and opportunity to kill Felix Muller. You've already lied several times in this investigation. We will hold you in our cells downstairs until I decide what to do with you.'

'I saw who killed Felix,' Zoe said suddenly.

'Say that again,' Clement said.

'I saw who killed Felix Muller.'

'Go ahead.'

'It was Mr Link – the man who owns that huge yacht on the harbour.'

'How do you know it was him?'

'I went to tell him that Felix was in the area, but he threw me out,' Zoe said, with bitterness. 'Then I saw his yacht following Felix's yacht back into port the next day, then Mr Link shot him with a rifle.'

'So, you went to see Mr Link, demanding money for information about Muller and he threw you out. In revenge, you've made up this unbelievable story about him shooting Muller,' Dupree said.

'It's not unbelievable. It's true, I tell you,' Zoe said indignantly.

'Take her away,' Clement called to a uniformed officer, who put handcuffs on her and led her away.

CHAPTER 37

After Zoe had been taken screaming down to the cells, the four detectives sat in Dupree's office to discuss the case. Dupree began the discussion. 'What do we think of her statement that Link killed Muller? She suddenly came up with it when I said we would hold her in our cells. She has a long criminal record. I don't believe a word she says.'

'I agree she is not an ideal witness,' Gould said. 'We would prefer a Sunday school teacher with a blameless life, but we don't have one of those around. I say we need to take her statement seriously and interview Edwin Link.'

'Apart from Zoe,' Philippa said, 'the German police couldn't find that Muller had many other friends in Berlin. So, I am confident he had no friends or associates with him when he arrived here.'

'We have been assuming that Muller is the kingpin in this case,' Gould said. 'Don't forget that the expedition would need a lot of money upfront and as far as we know Muller did not have much cash. Let's suppose he was working for a Mr Big who put Muller up for this expedition and then had him killed to make sure he couldn't talk or want more money. That would work, don't you think?'

'Yes, that would make sense,' Dupree said. 'But who is the Mr Big? Is he from Corsica or somewhere else?'

'I don't know but I have a feeling that some Corsican Mr Big would have to be involved, even if there was someone above him. That's where we have to rely on your local knowledge. Who has enough money and influence to fund this operation?'

'The local mafia springs to mind,' Dupree said. 'Everyone in

Corsica knows about Rommel's treasure and everyone, especially the Corsican Mafia, would love to get their hands on it. There have always been rumours that they found it long ago and have used it to fund their operations, but I doubt it. Someone within the Mafia would have boasted before now if they had found Rommel's treasure.'

'So, we have several believable theories,' Gould said. 'One is that Muller came to Corsica on his own initiative, hired a boat and crew, found the diamonds but a member of the crew then killed Muller. The other is that a Mr Big, probably a Corsican criminal, contacted Muller in Germany, persuaded him to come to Corsica, and funded the expedition. Then he terminated Muller's life as soon as he found the treasure.'

'The third is that Zoe killed Muller in some sort of crime of passion,' Clement said. 'In which case, we have the right person downstairs.'

'Then again some Corsican patriot could have recognised him and killed him in revenge for what he did in the war,' Gould said. 'That means everyone in Bastia that day is a suspect.'

'Perhaps Zoe was telling the truth,' Philippa said. 'Maybe Edwin Link killed Muller when he happened to recognise him on his yacht and grabbed his diamonds for selling in London.'

Dupree sighed. 'As always, we are not short of theories, but we need more evidence. The Mafia seem to be the strongest suspects so far. Santoni's family have been in charge of the local area for decades. I hope our visit the other day will make him do something reckless.'

'I say we need to interview Link and put Zoe's statement to him,' Gould said. 'I'd like to come with you, if you can arrange that, Anton.'

'I am sceptical about anything that Zoe says, but, yes, I agree we need to interview Edwin Link about the crime,' Dupree said, standing up to bring the meeting to a close.

CHAPTER 38

A few hours later, Dupree, Gould and Philippa stood on the jetty in the port at Bastia at the berth next to Edwin Link's yacht. Gould and Philippa gazed up and gasped. The vessel was even more impressive up close than it was when viewed from afar. The three police officers exchanged glances, all of them doubtless wondering how much money Link must have to afford such a vessel.

'This was the yacht I saw when my grandad and I were here earlier this year,' Philippa told Gould.

'That's right,' Dupree said. 'This Link character has been famous for hunting Rommel's treasure for several years. He comes every summer, but as far as I know he has never found anything.'

'If we are looking for a Mr Big to finance Muller's expedition, then Mr Link seems a strong candidate. Zoe's statement adds to the case against him. Perhaps she was telling the truth after all,' Gould said. He called up to a crew member leaning against the guard rail far above them. 'We are here to see Mr Link. My colleague is from the local police and we are from the City of London police,' he called, displaying his warrant card.

The crewman wandered off and returned a couple of minutes later. 'Mr Link will see you now,' the man called in an Eastern European accent. He ushered the three police officers on board and then along a corridor with walls lined with walnut wood. Eventually, they came to a door labelled 'Captain' and the crewman knocked.

'Come in,' came a man's voice from inside. The door was opened to reveal an elderly man standing up to greet them. His suit was expensively tailored, and overall, the police officers could tell that he had the pampered appearance of the very rich.

'I understand you are from the City of London police. You're a long way from home, but very welcome,' Link said in his slight Texan accent, offering to shake hands with them.

'I am Capitaine de Police Anton Dupree of the local police.'

'I am Detective Chief Inspector David Gould of the City of London's police,' Gould said, 'and this is my colleague Detective Sergeant Cottrell. We are investigating the death of a man in Bastia harbour on 30 May. Perhaps you could answer some questions for us.'

'Certainly, take a seat,' Link said, with exquisite politeness. 'I don't know anything about a murder, but I am happy to help you.'

'We understand that you have been involved in searches for what is known as Rommel's treasure for the past few years,' Philippa said.

'I have indeed. With little success so far, I'm afraid to say,' Link replied, with a rueful half-smile. 'As you may know, I made a good deal of money from inventing a trainer for pilots. As a result, I can afford to indulge this hobby every summer. It gives me an excuse to visit this beautiful part of the world.'

'I imagine you have done your research and have come across the name of Felix Muller,' Philippa said.

'Muller? The Beast of Bastia?' Link said. 'Of course. He was ordered to transport gold and diamonds from the North Africa campaign to Berlin. The treasure was never delivered there, and it is believed to have sunk off the coast of Corsica, but no one knows where. That is the basis of my search. I believe it is there, but, sadly, I have not found it yet. A lot of people say it is a fairy tale. They could be right, but I prefer to believe it is out there somewhere.'

'And do you know what happened to Felix Muller?' Dupree asked.

'No, it's a mystery,' Link said. 'He probably died at some stage during the war. At least, no one has seen him since.'

'That is where you are wrong, sir,' Philippa said. 'We have evidence that Muller was seen in Corsica recently and was murdered near here around a month ago.'

Link looked shocked. 'My God, that's a surprise, Philippa. May I call you Philippa?'

'Go ahead.'

'He would presumably know more than anyone else about Rommel's treasure. He would be an ideal source of information. It is a pity he is no longer around.'

'We are worried that he did in fact find some of the treasure and someone is now selling the diamonds on the London market,' Gould said, keeping his eyes fixed on Link's face. 'Do you know anything about that?'

'Not at all,' Link said. 'If you are right, I would love to know where he found them. Or if any diamonds are still left,' he added with a slight smile.

'It is very strange that you have not heard the rumours about Muller recently being alive, Mr Link. We have interviewed a young woman called Zoe Vogel,' Dupree said. 'She says she gave you information about Muller's whereabouts, but you said you didn't believe her. You then had her escorted off your yacht. Yet you claim to believe that Muller died in the war. Can you explain that?'

Link paused, apparently lost in thought, for a while. 'Oh, yes, there was a young woman who came on board and raved that she lived with Muller and he was now here in Bastia. She looked very scruffy. I didn't believe her and threw her out.'

'Then the next day, Muller was found murdered in the harbour,' Gould said. 'Miss Vogel told us she saw someone from this yacht killing him. Are you sure there is nothing you wish to add to your earlier statement?'

'No, I wouldn't believe anything that Vogel woman said. Perhaps she killed Muller herself. I wouldn't put anything past her, by the look of her,' Link said.

'We are considering conducting a re-enactment of the murder to try to jog people's memories,' Gould said. 'Would you be happy to cooperate if we did that?'

'Of course,' Link said. 'As I said, I would be happy to help the police in solving any crimes – even the murder of someone as vile as Felix Muller.'

'So, you do know something of Muller's wartime record?' Gould asked.

'Indeed, I do,' Link said. 'Considering the terrible way he treated the locals during the war, I recommend you consider anyone in Corsica over a certain age a suspect for Muller's murder. As I say, I always assumed he was dead a long time ago and know nothing of his recent history.'

'If you cannot help us any more, we will leave you now, Mr Link,' Dupree said, passing Link his business card. 'If anything should come up, please let me know on that number.'

'I should add there is a large reward for information leading to the identity of whoever is selling these diamonds,' Gould said.

'The reward would mean nothing to me,' Link said, indicating his palatial office, 'but I will be sure to keep you informed if I find out anything.'

Gould, Dupree and Philippa shook hands with Link, as he showed them off his yacht. As they arrived back on the jetty, Gould turned to Dupree and Philippa. 'Do you think we learnt anything from that visit?'

'No. Only how the rich live,' Philippa replied, with a rueful smile.

'Link knows a lot more than he told us,' Gould said. 'For one thing, how did he know your first name is Philippa? I never said it.'

'Yes, that's true. You just introduced me as Detective Sergeant Cottrell,' Philippa said, after a moment's thought. 'I wonder if he has contacts in the police who are keeping him informed of our inquiries.'

159

'We need to keep an eye on Mr Link,' Dupree said. 'Just imagine it. Spending loads of money and years of time on a fruitless search for a fortune. Then he hears that the person who originally had the money is alive, then suppose he sees him walking past your yacht. What would you do?'

'I'd be sure to make myself known to him,' Philippa replied. 'I'd tell him how much money I have. Then perhaps make Muller the proverbial offer he couldn't refuse.'

'And if Muller wouldn't say where the treasure was …' Gould suggested.

'I might be tempted to kill him, or at the very least, follow him to see where he went. Do you think Link might have killed Muller?' Dupree asked.

'It's possible,' Gould said. 'He would be a hero to many Corsicans if he did, but in the eye of the law, he would be a murderer.'

'I might be inclined to shake Link's hand as well,' Philippa said, 'if he killed Muller and if it was Muller who killed my grandfather, which looks almost certain.'

'There's another possibility,' Gould said. 'Perhaps Link met up with Muller as soon as he left East Germany, and Link provided funds to let Muller go to London and torture your grandfather. He then kills Muller as a result of some sort of quarrel among thieves. If that were true, Link is the Mr Big and behind the sale of the diamonds in London.'

'That would make sense to me,' Philippa said.

'I suggest we organise the re-enactment we've proposed as soon as we can, and watch Link's reaction,' Dupree said.

* * * *

After escorting Gould, Dupree and Philippa off his yacht, Link returned to his office, and knocked on one of the wooden doors. 'You can come out, now, Colonel.'

Christopher Davies walked out of the cabin where he had been hiding. 'They were the two British police officers I've been telling you about,' he said.

'So that's Philippa Cottrell,' Link said, 'the granddaughter of the man who sank the missing diamonds all those years ago. It's a pity I didn't know about William Cottrell earlier. He might have been a useful source of information for my search. Thank you, Colonel, you have been very useful,' Link added, passing a large bunch of US dollars to Davies.

'Thank you very much,' Davies said. 'That should help my pension nicely. You know, people like Gould laugh at historians like us. They say we live in ivory towers, studying ancient documents for no good reason. They don't realise that our information can be very valuable to the present.'

Link passed Davies a glass of whisky and they toasted the initial success of their joint plot.

CHAPTER 39

Tuesday was to be the day of the police re-enactment of Muller's murder. Three officers were ready to sail Muller's yacht into the harbour when Dupree gave the order. Other officers were stationed around the harbour to interview passers-by to see if they had seen anything of the murder a month before.

Gould, Philippa and Karl arrived to watch developments. 'You'd better stay away from us, Karl,' Gould said. 'We don't want Dupree to know who you are or about your interest in the case.'

'I'll do that. I'll keep an eye on things from over there,' Karl said, indicating a far corner of the harbour.

A few minutes later, Dupree arrived in his police car. He opened the door for Zoe to walk out. She looked scared, accompanied as she was by an unsmiling female police officer. Gould and Philippa walked up to Dupree.

'Is everything ready, Anton?' Gould asked.

Dupree seemed startled, and less than pleased to see the two British police officers. 'Ah, David and Philippa. I wasn't expecting you so early. Yes, everything is ready. We have three officers on the boat that Paulu said Muller had hired. We need to check Zoe's story. We've asked Link to stay on board his yacht.' He picked up his walkie-talkie. 'OK, sail Muller's yacht into the harbour now,' he ordered the boat's crew.

Everyone waited for a few minutes until Muller's yacht appeared from around the cliffs and approached the harbour. 'Is this how it was, Zoe?' Dupree asked sharply.

'Yes, that's right. The big yacht was following it.'

'Are you sure? Mr Link said it didn't move all that day,' Dupree asked. 'You'll be in trouble if you lie again.'

Zoe looked too frightened to reply at first. Gould wanted to suggest to Dupree he would get better results if he treated Zoe more sympathetically, but he reminded himself Dupree was the local police officer with all the authority. Gould and Philippa were only here with the agreement of Dupree. Somehow Gould knew that the cooperation could be swiftly withdrawn if he interfered with the way Dupree was running the investigation.

'I said are you sure, Fräulein Vogel.'

'Yes, I'm sure. Then that old man on the big yacht shot Felix in the back,' Zoe said.

'Did he shoot him with a gun?'

'Yes, a gun or a rifle, I'm not sure of the difference.'

'Muller was shot with a harpoon, not a gun or a rifle,' Dupree said. 'You're wasting our time, aren't you, Fräulein Vogel?'

Zoe looked embarrassed and scared. 'I thought it was a gun, perhaps I was wrong.'

Dupree spoke to the female police officer escorting Zoe. 'Take her away and put her back in the cells. I'll talk to her tomorrow.'

After Zoe was led away, Dupree turned to Gould. 'I can't see her as a valuable witness,' he said, then added after a thought. 'Mind you, she could be a viable suspect. I could see her killing Muller in a jealous rage – or if someone paid her to do it.'

By this time, Muller's yacht had slowly approached the docks close to where it had been found. A man of around Muller's build was standing on the deck.

'So, we think Muller was killed with a harpoon around there,' Dupree said. 'Then he either fell directly into the water or fell to the deck and was then pushed or kicked overboard. All this happened in the middle of the afternoon, yet no one saw anything useful. How are you getting on with any witnesses?'

'No one saw anything, M. Le Capitaine,' Clement said. 'We're not getting any useful information. When they learn the identity of the victim, they all smiled and said they hoped Muller rotted in hell.'

'He probably will, but we still need to find who killed him,' Dupree said. 'What do the forensics say? How far away was Muller from the killer when the harpoon entered his chest?'

'Around a metre. So, the killer was probably on the boat with him or on the quay as it was docking. That implies it was either Paulu or this Walter character he told us about.'

Dupree made a derisory gesture. 'This Walter who no one else has seen.'

'The forensics show the fingerprints of Paulu and Muller, as you expect.'

'But what about this Walter?'

'It's difficult because the yacht was hired by many different people this summer. But the latest fingerprints are those belonging to Paulu and Muller. There weren't any others where you would expect them to be.'

'So, no sign of this elusive Walter character.'

'No, sir. But if the yacht had come close to the dock, the killer could have been on the shore when he fired.'

'So, it could be Link, if he left the yacht and walked over to see what Muller was up to,' Dupree said. 'The only thing we can be sure of is that it didn't happen the way Zoe Vogel told us, so she is definitely lying, either to blackmail Link or to hide her own involvement.'

'If I may, Anton,' Gould said. 'The fact that the diamonds Muller found are now being traded in London points to a more serious criminal – either Walter, whatever his real name is, or Link or one of his crew. I can't see Paulu or Zoe having the knowledge to sell diamonds in London.'

'You may be right,' Dupree said. 'I still think both Paulu and Zoe must be considered suspects.' Dupree turned to Clement. 'Now, we've been filming the harbour all day, haven't we?'

'Yes, we've had seven men filming all the people watching the re-enactment. Most of them are just hangers on – we've been publicising it all week, so everyone knows about it.'

'Good, we'll look at the videos of all the people watching,' Dupree said. 'I'm prepared to bet the killer is here today. I know if I was the murderer, I'd come to watch the re-enactment to see how much the police knew and if I was in danger.'

'I've already spotted Santoni,' Clement said. 'You couldn't miss his Mercedes. Amelia Luri is here, as well.'

'OK, that's interesting, we'll interview them later. Let's get back to the scene of the crime. We think the body fell into the water about here, don't we?' Dupree said indicating the dock where they were standing.

'That's right, M. Le Capitaine,' Clement said. 'The body was found floating just near here, and it shouldn't have travelled far.'

'Bring Paulu Luri over here,' Dupree said. The detective brought a sulky Paulu up to Dupree.

'You're saying you were steering the boat,' Dupree said, 'yet you didn't see Muller being killed. That seems hard to believe.'

'That was the case, M. Le Capitaine,' Paulu replied. 'I was concentrating on steering the yacht. I carefully docked, then I called for the others to tie up the boat. I was annoyed when nothing happened. I came down to the dock and tied the boat up myself. Then I looked around, but there was no one here. They must have left just as we were docking. I waited a few minutes, then left the boat here. I thought my father and Walter had both left so they would not have to pay me any money.

'The rest is as I told you. The next day I approached the owner and told him to take his boat back. I never heard from Muller or Walter again.'

'Tell us more about Walter.'

'As I said, he had fair hair, but that could have been a wig. He had a slight foreign accent. He used to wear gloves all the time even when it was hot. Perhaps it was so he wouldn't leave any fingerprints.'

'So you say,' Dupree said. 'If you are right, Walter must have killed Muller and thrown his body into the water away from the dock and ran away while you were in the process of docking. Is there anything else you can tell us?'

'I saw some activity on that huge yacht.'

'Mr Link's yacht, yes?'

'If you say so, I think it was docking the same time as we were. I'm not sure, but I think it was following us.'

'But Mr Link says his yacht didn't move that day.'

'I can only say what I saw.'

'Do you know that young woman over there?' Dupree said, indicating Zoe in the back of the police car.

'No, I've never seen her before,' Paulu said.

'Her name is Zoe Vogel. She was your father's mistress in Berlin.'

'She means nothing to me,' Paulu said.

'OK, let's finish there,' Dupree said.

* * * *

Later at the station, Dupree turned to Clement. 'Let's look at the videos,' he said.

As they watched the pictures, Dupree saw Gould and Philippa, arriving with Karl. 'Who is that man?' Dupree asked. 'Someone I should know about?'

'Just a member of our team,' Gould said, embarrassed about having to lie.

'Who else can we see?'

'There's Amelia Luri.'

'We'll call her in. She'll say she was simply keeping an eye on her son but do it anyway.'

'Isn't that your Colonel Davies?' Clement asked, as they scrolled through the video.

Gould stared. 'Yes, it is.'

'Isn't he supposed to be in London?'

'Yes, he is. I'll have a word with him to see what he is doing here in Bastia.'

CHAPTER 40

In the early evening of the next day, Zoe was dozing in her cell when she was woken by some sort of commotion. As she woke up, she heard a rattling of keys and then saw a man walking towards her. At first, she was worried that some inmate was about to kill her, perhaps to ensure her silence about what she knew about Muller's murder. She gave a sigh of relief when she saw it was Dupree walking towards her. 'You may go now, Fräulein Vogel,' he said. 'I am not going to charge you with wasting police time, but I don't want to see you around Bastia again. I've had enough of your lies.'

'Don't worry, I won't be coming back here,' Zoe said, as she was taken from her cell and given her bag containing her few possessions back. After she left the police station, she walked along until she came to the quay area. She remembered this was where Felix Muller had been killed. She tried to rationalise her feelings over Muller's death. She knew that Karl had been right when he said that money was the only motivation for her to stay with an old man like Muller. Indeed, she told herself money was the main motivator for most of her actions, as it was for most people, she supposed, especially for those like herself who were poor.

Just then Zoe sensed someone following her along the road. Somehow, she had a sense of extreme danger. She ran toward the harbour, where she thought there might be more people and she would be safer. Immediately she took a detour into the same café where she had seen Amelia and Gash on the day of Muller's murder. Nobody followed her in, and she felt able to relax.

Zoe opened her bag, which she had no doubt the police had searched while she was in custody. She had told the police that

Felix Muller had not left any papers with him when he had left to go to Corsica. This was a lie and there was a hidden compartment in the bag where she had brought some documents that Muller had left behind. There was no sign that the Corsican police had discovered them. There were a few photos of Muller in Nazi uniform mostly with fellow soldiers, but the most interesting ones were several of Muller with an unknown woman. The two were pictured in domestic surroundings and it was obvious they were living as a couple.

Zoe studied the woman's face. Allowing for the passage of fifty years, Zoe was sure the lady in the old photograph was the woman who had the loud argument with the Englishman in this café on the day of Muller's murder. She felt if she could contact the woman – Zoe knew her name was Amelia, from the inscription on the back – she should be able to extract a substantial amount in blackmail. Zoe knew how unpopular the German occupiers had been during the war, and Amelia would want to keep her relationship with Muller secret to avoid a backlash from her neighbours. She guessed that the fact that Muller had been killed recently increased the value of these photos as a tool for blackmail.

Just then, Zoe saw a woman entering the café. She was sure she was the same woman. Once she had settled down, Zoe approached her.

'Pardon, madame,' Zoe said. 'I believe your name is Amelia.'

Amelia looked startled and affronted to be accosted by such a scruffy young woman. 'Who are you? What do you want?' she asked, looking around for someone to help get rid of Zoe.

'We have something in common, madame,' Zoe said. 'Or some person I should say – Felix Muller.'

'I don't know what you are talking about. Please leave me alone.'

'A month ago, I sat here while you shouted at some Englishman and accused him of murdering Felix. I was very interested because I knew Felix very well in Berlin. He left me some photos that you might like to have. Otherwise, I'm sure the local papers would give me money for them.'

Amelia peered at the old black and white photographs that Zoe showed her. Amelia's face dropped as she recognised a much younger version of herself with Muller during the war. 'How much do you want for these?'

'Just what you have in your wallet, madame,' Zoe said, then smiled as Amelia reluctantly gave her several hundred francs from her bag. Zoe passed Amelia the photos before the older woman rushed out of the café.

After Amelia left, a man whom Zoe recognised entered and joined her at the table. 'Hello, Zoe,' he said. 'We meet again.'

'What do you want?' Zoe asked. 'Why are you following me?'

'I thought you might recognise me,' the man said.

'Of course, I recognise you,' Zoe said. 'I could tell the police I saw you murder Felix Muller.'

'Why haven't you already?' he asked.

'I thought you might make me a better offer,' Zoe said. 'When the police are involved, I can be very forgetful when I want to be. The more money I am offered, the more forgetful I can be.'

'I thought that would be the case. It is a bit public here. Where can we discuss the terms for your silence?'

'We could talk outside,' Zoe said. 'But I want to stay in the open. I am not going anywhere alone with you.'

'Don't worry,' the man said. 'We won't be alone.'

The man followed Zoe outside, but as soon as she reached the pavement, he took out a stiletto knife hidden under his jacket, and stabbed Zoe through the heart. It was too sudden for her to make a sound. The passers-by who saw her assumed Zoe was drunk as she fell down lifeless and took no notice of the murderer walking away. They walked past Zoe, enjoying their holiday visit to Bastia. They did not notice the blood seeping out of her body, and she died unnoticed.

* * * *

Early the following morning, David Gould was woken in his hotel room by the phone ringing by his bed. He picked it up, wondering who would wake him up at such an early hour. 'Gould,' he growled in his half-awake state.

'Dupree here,' the voice said. 'There's been another murder. You will want to come down to the harbour, straight away. I'm sure it's relevant to our inquiry.'

Gould was about to ask for more information, but Dupree had hung up. Dressing quickly, Gould left his hotel and took a taxi to the harbour. He looked round, then saw the familiar sight of uniformed policemen keeping back a crowd of people who were looking down at a tarpaulin. A naked female arm was exposed.

'I'm glad you could come, David,' Dupree said. 'It's important for you to be here. I'm afraid it's someone we both know.' Gould had a moment when he was worried the victim might be Philippa. Then Dupree pulled the top of the tarpaulin back to reveal the lifeless face of Muller's ex-girlfriend.

Gould recoiled in shock. 'My God, it's Zoe,' he said. 'The poor kid.' He paused as he recovered his composure. 'No matter what she did or how she made her money, she didn't deserve this. She was only young even though she seemed tough. I guess that's what years working as a hostess in bars does to you. We need to catch whoever did this. What can we say about how she died?'

'She was killed by a long stiletto knife. It would have killed her instantly.'

'Is there any chance it was a random killing? She had a dangerous lifestyle – she knew dangerous people. Any of them could have killed her for any reason.'

'I doubt it was a random killing,' Dupree said, shaking his head. 'There was no sexual assault, and there were several hundred francs in her handbag untouched.'

170

'I'm guessing it must have been someone who knew she was helping us with our inquiries and wanted to silence her. Did anyone recognise her while she was in your cells?'

'Not as far as I know. The murderer might have seen her by chance and recognised her as a potential witness and killed her, before she could testify.'

'It looks very much as if Zoe saw Muller's murder and could identify the killer, even if she lied about who that person was,' Gould said. 'If Muller's murderer did kill Zoe as well, that means that person is still around here and keeping an eye on what is going on.'

'I'm sure Link was watching the re-enactment very carefully from his yacht. If it was a rich man like Link or Santoni, he could pay for people to keep an eye on the harbour to see if anyone is getting too curious about Muller's murder and kill them,' Dupree said. 'That means they would probably have a perfect alibi for the time of the murder, even though they were responsible. But speculating is not going to get us anywhere. We'll see what the forensic people tell us. Let's hope our killer has made a mistake of some sort and there are fingerprints or DNA on any items close to the body.' He ordered Clement to take the body away.

CHAPTER 41

In Corte the following day, Amelia was about to start her evening meal when she heard the doorbell ring. Cursing inwardly, she went to the front door and opened it. She stood in shock when she saw who was there.

'Hello, madame,' Santoni said. 'It's a long time since we last met, but I'm sure you remember me.'

Amelia gasped. 'M. Santoni, of course I remember our last meeting. The whole of Corsica knows of you. But what is it? I have done nothing wrong.'

'We'll see about that. May I come in?' Santoni entered Amelia's house without waiting for a response and looked around. 'You have a nice house, Madame. I would hate to see anything happen to it.' Amelia stared at Santoni with hatred, but did not speak. 'I gather an old friend of yours visited you recently, Madame. Felix Muller, the Beast of Bastia.'

'Muller is no friend of mine. I told him to go away.'

'And what did he say to you during his visit?'

'Nothing at all.'

Santoni sighed and took a seat. 'You are a mature lady now, aren't you, madame. I am sure we both remember things that those who are younger never knew.'

'You should be glad of that,' Amelia said. 'A lot of what happened in the war should be forgotten.'

'I am sure you are glad to forget those days, madame,' Santoni said. 'You look like a harmless old lady now, but if the local hooligans knew you were a traitor during the war, they could make your life hell.'

'They already did. Thanks to you, the locals made my life hell for many years after the war was long over – even though you knew I was not a traitor.'

'Those days are gone,' Santoni said, 'I am sure you don't want any of that unpleasantness to start again. But I could make sure it does. I don't imagine you will survive being lynched at your current advanced age, do you?'

'You know I couldn't face all that again,' Amelia said, her voice trembling with fear.

'Let's hope it doesn't come to that. I will see myself out,' Santoni said, standing up. 'You know what to do, don't you? Just ask your son Paulu to come and see me and discuss what he has done with Rommel's treasure. That will avoid a lot of unpleasantness.'

* * * *

Amelia shook with rage once Santoni had left. She knew what people thought of her. For years after the war ended, people in the street had spat at her and called her a whore. The name calling had gradually ceased as the years passed, and she had become a respectable old lady.

But the catcallers of long ago and the patronisers of today both ignored one salient fact. Amelia was a highly intelligent woman. She knew a lot about Muller's activities. She knew he was trying to take valuables away from Corsica before the Allies landed. She did not know the exact location of the jewels but knew more than most people now alive.

Amelia wished to ensure a prosperous future for her son. She knew full well that Muller was the father of Paulu, her son. If he needed a little help in retrieving the treasure, she felt that was part of her role as a mother. She picked up her phone and dialled.

'Santoni's looking for you, Paulu,' she said, as soon as her son answered. 'We both know it won't be long until he finds you.'

Paulu sighed. 'Things are looking bad for us, Maman. Do you have the phone number those policemen gave you? I may need to go to see them.'

'That is the sensible thing to do.'

'But they will want to know who killed my father. It wasn't you, was it, Maman? I wouldn't blame you if you did.'

'No, of course, I didn't,' Amelia said, putting the phone down. Somehow, she did not think her son believed her.

CHAPTER 42

The next day, Paulu was walking down a side road in Bastia, when a battered Citroen stopped in front of him. Three large men climbed out of the car and stood in front of Paulu.

'Who the hell are you?' Paulu asked, looking around in vain for help from any source.

'Paulu Luri! M. Santoni wishes to see you,' the leader of the men said.

Paulu moved to one side. 'I have no wish to see him.'

'Perhaps you didn't hear us. We said Mr Santoni wishes to see you,' the leader said. 'Everyone knows he doesn't take no for an answer.'

Paulu looked round for a way of escape but could see none. He was bundled into the car. The men drove him up through narrow mountain roads to Santoni's villa. Once they were inside, Santoni came up to Paulu.

'I gather someone is selling stolen diamonds on the London market,' Santoni said, with an air of understated menace. 'I believe you are involved. I would like to know how you came to possess them.'

Paulu looked sulkily at Santoni. 'I am not saying anything.'

'Well, then let me answer my own question. I think your daddy is or was Felix Muller, the Beast of Bastia. Somehow the two of you found the missing Rommel treasure. I think you killed your father and are now busy selling diamonds in London. Do you know how that makes me feel? It gives me a new respect for you and your mother. And it also makes me want some of the loot.'

'I don't have any diamonds, Mr Santoni,' Paulu said, nervously.

Santoni paused and glared at Paulu. 'Do you know how much

175

of the crime in this area I control, Mr Luri?' Santoni asked, indicating the panoramic view from his veranda.

'No, Mr Santoni.'

'Nearly all of it, and I want it to stay that way,' Santoni said, coming up close to Paulu. 'You say you don't know who has the treasure. Somehow, I don't believe you. But I'm a reasonable man. I will let you go now. My people will pick you up after a week. At that time, I expect you to come up with a proposal to give me my share of the profits.' Santoni gave a smile as cold as ice. 'Do you know what happens to people who don't do what I say and operate on their own in Bastia?'

'No, Mr Santoni,' Paulu mumbled in fear.

'Believe me, you don't want to know. Nobody has ever lived to tell of it. I will see you in a week's time,' Santoni said, ushering for one of his henchmen to escort Paulu out of his villa. 'Don't try to hide, M. Luri,' Santoni said as Paulu was dragged out. 'I will find you, and I will kill you – if I am feeling merciful, that is.'

CHAPTER 43

That evening, an hour later after they had ordered their meals in a restaurant close to their hotel, Karl turned to Philippa. 'I've been meaning to say how sorry I am about your grandfather, Philippa,' he said, gently touching her hand. 'He seemed a fine man when I saw him in the distance that day when you were both on holiday.'

'Thank you, Karl, I appreciate that,' Philippa said, not moving her hand. 'I know old men have to die – it's natural. But he should have died comfortably in bed, not tied up to a piece of apparatus. Grandad didn't deserve to be killed like that – and I'm sure he was murdered. There's no way he would have killed himself, and it wasn't an accident.'

'If we can find the man who killed Muller, I hope we can persuade the London police he murdered your grandfather as well,' Karl said. 'The most hopeful possibility is to find whoever is selling the diamonds in London. I'm sure Dupree is involved, probably in a conspiracy with Santoni.'

'We've no proof Dupree is anything other than an honest cop.'

'An honest cop who does everything he can to obstruct your investigation,' Karl, said with a snort.

Philippa tried to move to more neutral topics. 'So, how did you get involved with Rommel's treasure, Karl?' she asked.

'At first it was just a case, like any other,' Karl replied. 'I thought it was ancient history that didn't matter much nowadays. Then it got under my skin. Just the idea that the rightful owners are dead, and their descendants living in poverty, makes my blood boil. The Nazis in the war are all dead now, but the modern criminals – probably the Mafia – now probably have Rommel's treasure. To make it worse, I'm sure Dupree, who is supposed to be investigating Muller's death, is being paid by them – probably by Santoni. Still, with any luck, we'll be able to find those jewels and pass them back to the rightful owners.'

Philippa gazed at Karl. She was reluctant to admit it, but his speech had impressed her. 'Do you think we can solve Grandad's murder, Karl?'

'I'm sure of it, Philippa.' Karl tossed Philippa a dog-eared paperback. She picked it up and saw it was *On Her Majesty's Secret Service* by Ian Fleming. Philippa looked at Karl as if he was mad. 'Why are you giving me this?'

'It's useful homework for this case. Do you know what Ian Fleming's job was in the Second World War?'

'No, I don't,' Philippa replied, wondering where this conversation was headed.

'He had a senior role in intelligence for the Royal Navy. A lot of the ideas for his James Bond novels came from those days. This one in particular was about smuggled gold in Corsica. Does that sound familiar?'

'It sounds like Rommel's treasure. It seems my grandfather was involved in smuggling Nazi treasure for real.'

'It does look like it,' Karl said, gazing at Philippa with sympathy.

Philippa could not suppress a smile when she thought of the contrast between her grandfather's terraced house and the fantasy world of Ian Fleming's novels. 'If so, I've no idea what happened to the money he received from selling the diamonds. I never saw any of it.'

'Are you sure, Philippa?'

Philippa thought. 'Perhaps we did have a bit more money than you might expect. My parents are dead now, and my grandparents brought me up. Grandad never seemed to be short of money, really. He just seemed an honest policeman. I know there were some crooked police officers in those days. I'm sure there still are some around, but I knew he wasn't one of them. A lot of his colleagues came to his funeral and they all said how much they respected him. I'd love to know what happened to the threatening letters he said he received. There's no sign of them in any of his possessions.'

At the end of the meal, Karl turned to Philippa 'Why don't we go back to your room and talk about it some more?' he asked.

Philippa gave a half-smile. She realised both of them knew this was a chat-up line and Karl was hoping to spend the night with her. Philippa had been hurt by her past breakup with David Gould and had promised herself not to become involved with fellow police officers again. Somehow, she felt any friendship with Karl would be different, but she told herself she was not ready for a relationship yet.

'Let's just go for a walk, shall we?' she asked. They walked along the harbour. Philippa did not object when Karl reached out to hold her hand.

CHAPTER 44

Two days later, Gould and Philippa joined Dupree in his office in Bastia police station. The Corsican officer was looking more downcast than the visiting City of London detectives had seen him so far. 'We've had the forensics back on the latest murder. It's bad news, I'm afraid. Whoever killed Zoe Vogel was an expert. There are no fingerprints anywhere on her body. The only DNA is hers. We haven't found the weapon but, from the wound, we know it is a stiletto knife. We haven't found any witnesses to the murder itself.

'The only slight lead is that the owner of the café saw Zoe come in and sit at the table. At first, she spoke to an unknown elderly woman, who looked Corsican. She seemed to give Zoe some money then left. Then a man came in and joined Zoe. The owner didn't get the impression Zoe was expecting him. The conversation didn't seem friendly. They didn't order any drinks and he remembered the man following Zoe outside. That was all.'

'Would he recognise this man if he saw him again?'

'He doesn't think so. The café was quite busy. He seemed to be a man in his thirties. They spoke in English, but that doesn't necessarily mean anything. It is the international language after all.'

'I wonder if he is this mysterious Walter that Paulu Luri talks about,' Gould said.

'It must be someone who has been following this investigation to know that Zoe was a potential witness.' Dupree thought for a moment. 'Unless they saw her talking to us during the re-enactment.'

'Zoe claimed she saw Edwin Link kill Muller. We always thought she was lying, but if she was telling the truth, perhaps Link killed her or ordered one of his crew to wield the knife.'

'You may be right, but we know Zoe was a liar. The fact that she is dead does not alter that fact,' Dupree said, with a dismissive gesture.

'Maybe so, but someone killed her and thought she must have known something they didn't want her to reveal. I'll have Philippa follow Link and see what we can find out,' Gould said.

'As you wish, Chief Inspector,' Dupree replied, his frostiness making it clear he felt following Link would be a waste of time.

CHAPTER 45

As instructed by Gould, Karl and Philippa watched Link's yacht from a nearby café. During the long hours of waiting, they gradually became better acquainted. After a while, the subject of relationships came up.

'So, is there anyone waiting for you at home, Philippa?' Karl asked.

'No, there hasn't been for a while. David Gould and I used to be close, but now we're just …' Philippa's voice tailed away.

'Just good friends?' Karl suggested, with a smile. 'Isn't that the English phrase?'

'No, I was going to say just colleagues. It's strange that it works, but it does,' Philippa said. 'And how about you? Do you have a wife and lots of children back home in Holland?'

'No, I never seem to have enough time. My life seems dedicated to finding the diamonds and gold the Nazis stole during the war. The fact that the thefts took place a long time ago doesn't affect how unjust it is for them or their successors to have such valuables. If I can recover at least some of them for the true owners, I'll be happy,' Karl said, then smiled. 'So, you see I seem a bit obsessed with work. There doesn't seem much time for relationships.'

'I think I understand how you feel. Police work tends to dominate our lives, doesn't it? Perhaps that's why police officers tend to marry each other,' Philippa said, then suddenly sat up straight. 'One moment, someone's leaving the yacht,' she added, looking through her binoculars. 'My God, it can't be.'

'Who is it?' Karl asked.

'It's Colonel Davies, our historical expert. So, it was him in the video of the re-enactment. What is he doing here? He said he was flying back to London.'

'Well, he's certainly in Corsica now, he seems to be doing his historical research in luxury on Link's yacht. Shall we follow him?'

'I'm inclined to tackle him face on,' Philippa said.

'Are you sure?' Karl asked.

'I'm sure,' Philippa said, instinctively touching Karl's hand before she realised she had done it. She walked out of the café and approached the man leaving the yacht. 'Colonel Davies,' she called.

Davies turned around, startled. 'Oh, Sergeant Cottrell.'

'What are you doing here? You said you were returning to London some time ago, Colonel – or Christopher, if you prefer.'

'I changed my plans. I wanted to do some more research while I am here.'

'What research would that be?' Philippa asked. 'Perhaps we could have a little chat? I will need to make a report on why you were seen leaving the company of a suspect in a murder case.'

'A suspect? Edwin Link is just a friend.'

'Mr Link is a very rich man who has spent a lot of time looking for Rommel's treasure. It would give him a motive to kill Felix Muller – the man who lost it all those years ago. Shall we go into this café? I have a colleague from Interpol there.'

Davies looked around as if planning an escape but nodded and followed Philippa into the café.

'This is Karl Jansen from Interpol,' Philippa said.

'How do you do, Colonel?' Karl said, shaking Davies's hand. 'I'm a fan of yours. I enjoyed your book on Rommel's treasure.'

'Thank you. I'm glad you enjoyed it,' Davies said, joining the two police officers at the table.

'Yes, indeed,' Karl continued. 'It is required reading in my section of Interpol. We have been trying to find the treasure and restore it to its rightful owners.'

183

'Yes, it is a fascinating period of history,' Davies said, with the zeal of an academic discussing their favourite subject.

'But for me and my family, it is not just history, is it, Colonel?' Philippa asked. 'I very much suspect Felix Muller killed my grandfather to find the yacht with the valuables he stole which sank back in 1943.'

'Yes, I know, Philippa. I'm sorry for your loss, but ...'

'You could tell us, Colonel,' Karl said, 'what you were talking with Link about on his yacht.'

'I don't have to tell you that,' Davies said, raising his voice in indignation.

'Perhaps not,' Philippa said, 'but I would have to report back that you were obstructing our inquiries. You may also have been offending under the Official Secrets Act. You are a serving army officer. I'm not sure how all that would go down with your seniors.'

Davies sat down, deflated. 'Oh, very well. The truth is I approached Link recently to help him with his searches. I had information that Muller was interrogated by the Russians after the war. I only found out about it because I speak Russian. I knew what he said then might help Link's searches.'

'What did Muller say in the interrogation?' Karl asked.

'He admitted being in Corsica but made sure he seemed like an ordinary foot soldier, following orders. He did offer to help recover some Nazi treasures if the Russians would reduce his time as a prisoner of war.'

'And did the Russians take him up on his offer back then?'

'It seems not. I don't think the colonel interrogating him believed him. Muller did say the treasure was not far from Bastia.'

'And did Edwin Link find the information you provided useful?'

'Yes, it seems that although Muller did not know exactly where the treasure was, he was closer than everyone else. He may have tortured your grandfather so he could be more precise as to where it exactly was.'

'The obvious thing was to pass this information onto DCI Gould and myself, who you knew were investigating a murder. Instead, you used the knowledge you gained as an army officer to help Link, who may well have been involved in murder. All to line your own pocket. That does not seem to be the action of an officer and a gentleman, Colonel,' Philippa said.

Davies looked ashamed, as he left the café and walked along the quay away from Philippa and Karl.

CHAPTER 46

The next day, Clement entered Dupree's room in Bastia police station, where Dupree and Gould were discussing progress on the case.

'Capitaine, Paulu Luri has come to the front desk. He says he wishes to make a statement.'

'That's very interesting,' Gould said. 'I wonder if the re-enactment scared him at all.'

'We will see,' Dupree said. 'You are welcome to take part in the interview. How shall we approach it?'

'Do you know the expression – hard cop, soft cop?'

'I think so. Which are you going to be?'

'I'll be soft cop,' Gould said. 'I think we'll get more from him that way.'

Dupree shrugged. 'Let Paulu in. I would like you here to take notes.'

'Yes, Capitaine,' Clement said. He returned within a minute, ushering Paulu to take a seat.

Paulu sat in the interrogation room across the table from Dupree and Gould. Clement took notes at a separate table. 'I wish to make a statement,' Paulu said. 'I believe my life is in danger, and I request police protection.'

'You gave a statement to us a week ago,' Dupree said, in an unwelcoming tone.

Paulu looked embarrassed. 'I wish to – clarify a few things.'

'You mean you lied before. How do we know if you are telling the truth now?' Paulu looked embarrassed but did not reply. 'Go ahead, M. Luri. I should make it clear we will make a record of whatever you tell us,' Dupree continued. 'If necessary, we may need to prosecute you.'

186

Paulu took a deep breath. 'Let me start from scratch and tell the full story. As you know, recently I took part in a mission to retrieve stolen German diamonds. My father is or was Felix Muller – the Beast of Bastia. I only knew him by his reputation as a man people were scared of during the war. We met for the first time when he returned to the island recently.'

'Was this when he visited your mother?' Gould asked.

'That's right. I overheard them talking and followed Muller to Bastia. At first, I was horrified when my mother told me he may have been my father. Then I thought I would turn it to my advantage and try to get some money from him. I knew he was looking for treasure from the war that was buried at sea, so I offered to crew for him. I had crewed on yachts in the past so I told him I could be useful to him. I knew he had no reason to trust me, but perhaps the thought that I might be his son persuaded him. Anyway, he agreed for me to crew, but brought along a third crew member – a man called Walter. I don't know very much about him. The two of them said they had obtained new information that should help them find the diamonds.'

'What information was that?' Dupree asked, exchanging glances with Gould.

'I don't know. Perhaps they dug up some old documents, but I think they probably extracted it from someone who was involved back in 1943. I hate to think what they did to the person to persuade them to pass over information. I know my father wasn't afraid to kill, if he felt the need.'

'We're investigating the murder of an old British soldier in London recently. We think Muller may have been involved,' Gould said. 'Did they mention the name Bill Cottrell at all?'

'No,' Paulu said, slowly. 'I've never heard that name, but I'm sorry if he was killed.'

'So, what can you tell us about this man who called himself Walter?'

Paulu took a deep breath and continued. 'My father and Walter took turns diving – looking for treasure, of course. That final day went as usual. When they had finished, I sailed the yacht back to the harbour. When I was about to dock, I called for them to tie up, but there was no reply. I managed to bring the yacht in and tied it up myself. I shouted, "Why the hell didn't you help?" but when I looked around the deck, my father and Walter were both missing. I was baffled, but I assumed they had found some diamonds and decided to leave me there so they wouldn't have to share any of the loot with me. I wouldn't trust either of them, to be honest with you.

'I sailed the yacht back to the owner the next day. I got a couple of friends to crew for me. I don't know what happened to my father and Walter. It meant I was left unpaid for the sailing I did. Now Santoni's men are threatening me. They seem to think I have Rommel's treasure – whatever that is. They're following me wherever I go. I'm worried for my life and am asking you to protect me.'

Dupree spoke aggressively to Paulu. 'I don't believe your story. I suggest you killed your father to get hold of all the diamonds. I don't believe this Walter exists. I suggest he's a made-up person that you can blame for your father's murder. Now you are selling the diamonds he found. What do you say to that?'

'It's not true,' Paulu replied, looking to Gould for help. 'I never murdered anyone, and I don't have any diamonds. I wouldn't hang around in Corsica if I did,' Paulu continued. 'There was one odd thing about Walter – he always wore gloves even in the heat of the summer.'

'That seems suspicious,' Gould said.

'Do you think he was trying to avoid leaving fingerprints? That's what I would do if I knew I was going to murder someone.'

'We didn't find any recent fingerprints on the yacht apart from yours and Muller's.'

'Do you think that means Walter was in the police and knew all about how to avoid leaving fingerprints?' Paulu asked, excitedly.

'I put it to you that Walter doesn't exist, Paulu,' Dupree replied. 'Or if he does exist, he has been watching real-life crime TV programmes too much and knows all about fingerprints. If Muller did find Rommel's treasure, the diamonds are not on the yacht you hired. Perhaps you killed Muller – who may or may not have been your father – and stole the diamonds yourself,' Dupree said.

'Why didn't you report your father as missing?' Gould asked, trying to move the interrogation on.

'I didn't think he would want to be found. I assumed he was away somewhere enjoying spending money from selling the diamonds.'

'A young woman named Zoe Vogel was murdered near Bastia harbour two days ago,' Dupree said. 'Do you know anything about her murder?'

'No, is that the woman you pointed out?'

'Yes, that was Zoe,' Dupree nodded.

'No, I'd never heard of her before then,' Paulu replied, looking bewildered.

'I can tell you what happened to your father,' Dupree said. 'He was killed by a harpoon gun in Bastia harbour. Walter is missing. We believe Walter, if he exists, killed your father to keep the diamonds to himself and is selling them in London.'

'I suspected something like that,' Paulu said. 'I won't mourn my father. He was an evil man, and I barely knew him. But will Santoni believe me if I say I don't have the diamonds?'

'We know all about Santoni. He is a dangerous man, and, no, I don't think he will believe you,' Dupree said. 'We believe your life is in danger.'

'Excuse us, Paulu, I need to talk to my colleague privately,' Gould said, indicating for a surprised Dupree to follow him into the corridor.

'What's going on, David?' Dupree asked. 'What do you want to talk about?'

189

'I'd like to continue this investigation in London, Anton.'

Dupree stared at Gould. 'Why's that? The murders of Felix Muller and Zoe Vogel occurred here in Bastia – my jurisdiction.'

'Yes, but William Cottrell was killed in London and the sale of the diamonds was there. There's also one major suspect in London I want to interview.'

'Who's that?'

'I want to find this sergeant who Amelia thinks betrayed Bill Cottrell back in 1943. If I can track him down, he should have interesting tales to tell.'

Dupree sighed dubiously and he stared at Gould as if wondering how far to trust him. 'I've tried to cooperate with you, David, but this seems very unorthodox to me.'

Gould continued to make his case. 'I'm also worried that Paulu Luri's life is in danger if he stays in Corsica and Santoni finds out he's cooperating with us. I want to take Paulu Luri and his mother back to London – away from Santoni's threats.'

After a long pause, Dupree gave a typically Gallic shrug of his shoulders, 'Very well, I'll agree, but keep me in touch. I'd like Sergeant Clement to follow you to London. He's familiar with the case and should be able to help you – and he'll make sure I'm informed of developments.'

Gould hesitated before continuing. 'Yes, I agree, having Clement in London might be useful, but I want to keep his involvement a secret – not even Philippa Cottrell must know. If she asks, make up some story that he is on leave in London.'

'I won't ask why, David, but I agree,' Dupree said. 'We'll shake hands on it. You know, David, I'm putting my career on the line for you by doing this. Just make sure I know about all the developments.'

'Don't worry, Anton. If I'm right, I expect everything to come to a head in London soon. I'd like you to join me – it should be an exciting conclusion.'

* * * *

After their discussion in the corridor, Gould and Dupree returned to the interview room. Paulu sat where they had left him, obviously baffled by the two detectives' sudden disappearance. Clement seemed as puzzled as Paulu was.

'If you want us to believe in the existence of this Walter and that you're innocent, you will need to cooperate with us,' Gould said. Paulu gave a frightened nod of acceptance. 'I need you to come to London and take part in an exercise for me. You are to offer to sell diamonds to a particular dealer in London. The pretend diamonds will be cut glass and so worthless, of course. Will you do that for me? Otherwise, Capitaine Dupree may have to arrest you for the murder of your father and the theft of diamonds, and possibly the murder of Bill Cotterill in London as well.'

'But I've never been to London and never owned any diamonds,' Paulu said, looking around in bewilderment.

'To be honest, I believe you,' Gould replied, 'but, as you see, Capitaine Dupree doesn't, do you, Anton?'

Dupree glared at Paulu. 'I need to make an arrest for the murder of Felix Muller and Zoe Vogel, and I'm looking at the prime suspect.'

'So you see, I am the only friend you have. If you can't cooperate with me, at the moment, it looks as if you could be charged with conspiracy to steal a large number of diamonds. You would receive a long prison sentence. You would be prime suspect for your father's murder. If you go to prison, one of Santoni's men inside will be sure to attack and possibly kill you for the diamonds, even if you don't have them. Does any of that appeal to you?'

'No, of course, it doesn't,' Paulu said. 'Just tell me what I have to do.'

'I have arranged an exercise in London to uncover the real murderer. Are you willing to play your part?'

191

'Yes, sir.'

Gould turned to Dupree. 'I want to take this man to London with me. His life is in danger here. Do you agree?'

Dupree shrugged. 'As long as you don't lose him. As far as I'm concerned, he is still a suspect for the murder of Muller in my jurisdiction.'

Gould turned to Paulu. 'As you can see, your life is in danger from the Mafia here. If they don't kill you, Capitaine Dupree has a cell waiting for you. The only alternative is coming with me to London, but it will mean a permanent change to the lives of you and your mother ...' Gould outlined some of the rest of his plan to a staggered Paulu.

CHAPTER 47

Gould left the police station and returned to his hotel. He packed his bags, picked up Philippa, and drove his hired car to Corte, where, as arranged, Clement had brought Paulu.

'Thank you for your help, Sergeant,' Gould said.

'Good luck with your exercise, Inspector,' Clement said, before driving back to Bastia. 'Perhaps we'll meet up in London.'

'Are you ready, Paulu?' Gould asked.

'I'm ready – nervous, but ready. I don't know how my mother will react, though.'

'Let's find out, shall we?' Gould said, as they approached Amelia Luri's house. He indicated for Paulu to wait out of sight, as he knocked on the front door.

'What do you want now?' Amelia asked in extreme annoyance, holding the door open halfway. 'I've told you everything I know.'

'There have been important developments, which I need to tell you about, Madame. To start with, I've brought your son home,' Gould said, ushering Paulu forward. 'He has made a statement to the police, which we found very interesting. He claims he has now told us the truth, after lying in his first statement. Perhaps you could start telling us the truth too. First of all, your son has something to tell you.'

'You know I've been threatened by Santoni, Maman,' Paulu said. 'He's threatened to kill me if I don't give him some of Rommel's diamonds. We both know he would do it if I don't cooperate, but I don't have anything to give him. So, I've requested the police to give me protection. Mr Gould has a proposal to make to you.'

'Exactly so,' Gould said. 'The lives of you and your son are in danger, Madame Luri. I am offering you a way out if you help us with our inquiries into the murders of Felix Muller and William Cottrell as well as a young woman in Bastia. I want you to fly with me to London and help us trap their killer. Whoever he is, we know he is extremely dangerous – he has already killed at least three people. You must understand you and your son's lives are in danger if you stay here. If you come to London and help me uncover the source of the diamonds, you and your son should be in line for a large reward.

'I realise this will be a shock, but the good news is that you and your son will be able to start a new life somewhere else. The bad news is it may not be safe for you to live in Corsica anymore. The reward money should help you to relocate – probably somewhere in mainland France.'

Amelia looked horrified. 'So, you're saying that I have to leave my own home, even though I have done nothing wrong. Why can't the guilty people leave Corsica instead of us innocent people? No, I won't leave here,' she finished, stamping a foot.

'Please, Maman,' Paulu said. 'This is the only way out. Santoni will kill both of us if we stay on this island.'

'Do you think Santoni is behind these murders?' Amelia asked.

'We are not sure, but he is one of the main suspects we wish to investigate,' Gould said.

'Whoever the murderer is, we need to have you and your son moved to safety,' Philippa intervened.

'You will need to move now, Madame Luri,' Gould said. 'I believe I know who the killer is, but I need you to cooperate with me, if we are to make a case against him. I will arrange for two plane tickets to London, and I'll make sure you will be safe there.'

Amelia looked around her front room. 'This is my home. I was born here. Why should I have to leave?' she asked, her eyes full of tears.

'Please, Maman. I don't want either of us to die,' Paulu said.

Amelia gazed at Paulu for a long time, then sighed. 'Oh, very well. I'll cooperate,' she said.

Paulu rushed forward and hugged his mother. 'Thank you, Maman. We're doing the right thing.'

'There are still some things I would like to know, Madame Luri,' Gould said. 'Despite what you told us, I believe Felix Muller came to see you this year. Is that correct?'

Amelia paused before answering. 'Yes, he did visit me. I am sorry I lied to you before.'

'Before then, when was the last time you saw Felix Muller, Madame Luri?'

'In 1943 – just before the American troops arrived in Corsica. I knew Felix had either escaped with the rest of the Germans or had been killed. I thought I was free then, but in some ways, it got even worse,' Amelia said, before continuing with a shudder. 'After the Resistance people came to Corte, the local women dragged me out, stripped me and cut all my hair off. Then they dragged me through the streets and jeered at me. The leader of them was Santoni, who is forcing us off the island now, and everyone knows what he is capable of. The women called me a whore, but, believe me, most of them were no better than me.'

'We are sorry for what you went through, Madame. You didn't deserve any of it,' Philippa said. 'My grandfather said you helped him right until he was captured. We know you were a hero back in 1943.'

'Nobody of your age could know what life was like then,' Amelia said, gazing at Philippa with something close to contempt. 'I did what I thought was right for Corsica.'

'Tell us more about Muller's visit this year,' Gould said. 'We do need to know where he went when he left you. It might help us find out who killed him.'

'He said he was going to Bastia, looking for Rommel's diamonds, and wanted help. I told him I didn't want to see him again, and he left.'

'Just one thing to satisfy my curiosity, Madame,' Philippa said. 'If you did not betray my grandfather in 1943, do you know who did?'

Amelia's expression softened. 'I am sorry Bill Cottrell was killed. He was a good man. But anyone could have seen him visit me during the war and told the Germans. In particular, he had a sergeant I did not trust. I think he may have betrayed Bill.'

Philippa thought for a moment. 'Was the sergeant's name Gash, by any chance?'

'Yes, Tony Gash was his name. I never trusted him. I saw him talking to some German officers during the war once, which looked suspicious. I'm sure he betrayed your grandfather to Felix.'

Philippa nodded. 'That is very useful information – we will follow that up. Thank you, madam.'

'There is one other thing you will be interested in knowing,' Amelia said. 'I saw Tony Gash not long ago in Bastia. I believe it was the day Felix was killed.'

'Tony Gash?' Philippa asked. 'My grandfather's sergeant during the war? He was here in Corsica? That's extraordinary. Are you certain it was him?'

'Yes, I'm sure,' Amelia said. 'It was in a café overlooking the jetty. He denied killing Muller, but I suggest you interview him. His behaviour seemed very suspicious to me.'

'You say you spoke to Tony Gash about Muller's murder? The murder you claimed to know nothing about?' Gould asked.

Amelia shrugged. 'I've said before I did not tell the truth last time you visited. I'll admit now I was in Bastia when Felix was murdered – but I did not do it. I didn't see who killed him, so I don't know who did. But I know neither Paulu nor I murdered Felix Muller.'

'We'll have to see about that,' Gould said. 'Please get ready to leave now. We must catch the next flight to London to get you to safety. There's one other thing, did either of you see this young woman in Bastia? She was found murdered.' Gould showed Paulu then Amelia a photo of Zoe.

Paulu shook his head. 'I saw her at the re-enactment but not before then. I'm sorry if she was killed, but that was the only time I saw her.'

Amelia nodded. 'Yes, I did see her in a café in Bastia harbour the day after the re-enactment. She had some old photos of me with Felix and threatened to show them to the press. I gave her some money from my bag to keep her quiet then. I don't know who killed her, though.'

'You both seem to have been close to the scene of the crime when two recent murders took place,' Gould said. 'You are either very unlucky or that might seem suspicious. At first sight, either of you could be a suspect in both murders.'

Amelia shrugged. 'Think what you like, Chief Inspector. I can only tell you I didn't kill either Felix or the girl in the café.'

Gould said. 'I will believe you for the time being, but it is essential you come to London with us. I want you to cooperate with us so we can find the real murderer.' Amelia nodded agreement. 'Very well, please pack as much as you need. I will arrange a flight to London for you and your son.'

An hour later, Amelia and Paulu joined Gould and Philippa in their car to catch a flight from Bastia airport to London. As they drove through the mountains, they did not notice that a motorcycle ridden by one of Santoni's thugs followed them to the airport. He spotted which plane the party were booked onto, and immediately phoned Santoni, telling him of Paulu's travel plans. The thug took care to speak in the Corsican language, which he knew few in the police could speak, to add to the secrecy.

Gould turned to Philippa. 'I want you to stay here in Bastia, Philippa. Keep an eye on Link and use your initiative if anything else comes up on the case. I've asked Dupree to let you know what's happening. I'll tell you when I need you and Karl back in

London. Don't worry, I'll make sure you're around when we wrap up this case.'

'Sure thing, gov. I'd love to know how your interview with Tony Gash goes. I'm suspicious of him. I'm guessing he betrayed Grandad back in 1943, and knows something about the murders since,' Philippa replied as she left Gould, Amelia and Paulu at the airport for their flight to London.

* * * *

After a two hour flight, Gould, Amelia and Paulu arrived at Heathrow. Detective Sergeant Fox, a long-standing member of Gould's team, was there to pick them up. Gould smiled as the two Corsicans complained about the mild temperature, which seemed cold to them. The drive to the centre of town in the police car was more like a tourist trip as Gould and Fox described the London sights to the Corsican visitors.

Eventually, the police car arrived at a one-star hotel near the City. None of the people in the car realised they had been followed from the airport by a motorcycle ridden by a member of a London criminal gang, who owed Santoni a favour. The motorcyclist made a note of the hotel and passed the information to his boss, who, in his turn, ensured that Santoni knew where Paulu and Amelia were staying in London.

Once Gould and Fox had left Amelia and Paulu at the hotel, they made their way to Snow Hill police station. Gould brought Fox up to date with the developments in the Corsican diamonds case. Gould handed his sergeant a name. 'Find me this man's address. All I know is that he is an old soldier in the same regiment as Bill Cottrell, Philippa's grandfather. He is a suspect in this case and I very much want to pay him a visit.'

CHAPTER 48

Two days later, Tony Gash heard the doorbell ring at the door of his Beckenham home. He had a sudden panic attack when he had a mental image of Muller making a return visit. After a moment, he remembered that Muller was dead, but there was still something threatening about the sound of the doorbell. When he opened the door, he was staggered when he saw Amelia accompanied by two official-looking men he did not recognise.

'Amelia?' Gash asked. 'What are you doing here? How did you find me? What do you want?'

'Mr Gash?' The man said, showing his warrant card. 'May we come in? I'm Detective Chief Inspector David Gould of the City of London police. This is my colleague Detective Sergeant Fox. Of course, you already know Amelia Luri.'

'What is this about?' Gash asked, looking genuinely baffled.

'Would you rather we discuss this outside, or may we come in?' Gould asked.

'You'd better come in,' Gash said, unwillingly ushering his visitors inside.

'I believe I saw you at Bill Cottrell's funeral, Mr Gash,' Gould said, when the visitors had sat down in Gash's sitting room. 'Philippa Cottrell is a friend and colleague of mine. It was terrible what happened to her grandfather.'

'Yes, I know all that, but why are you here now?'

'How did you come to know Bill Cottrell, Mr Gash?'

'I assume Amelia has told you,' Gash said. 'We were in Corsica during the war. I was a sergeant, and Bill was my commanding officer.'

'Please tell me what happened before Bill became a prisoner of war.'

Gash took a deep breath. 'On that last day, we organised a raid to kill Muller, the local Gestapo leader. But it went wrong. Cottrell was captured, but I managed to escape. A few days later, the Americans liberated the island and I returned home. But I don't know why you are asking about events of so long ago.'

'Can you add anything, Amelia?' Gould asked.

'It's not all in the past, as you well know, Tony. Bill came to see me not long ago,' Amelia said. 'He thought it was me who gave him away to Muller, but it wasn't. The only other person it could have been was you, Tony. I told Bill, and he seemed shocked. But in the end, I could tell he believed me. He realised you were the traitor.'

'She's lying. Amelia could have given Bill away,' Gash told Gould. 'She was sleeping with Muller at the time, after all. Who knows where her real loyalties were?'

'One matter at a time, please,' Gould said, before Amelia could reply. 'Now, Mr Gash, tell me the truth – when did you last see Bill Cottrell?'

'He came to see me earlier this year. I assumed it was for a friendly chat about the old days,' Gash said. 'But then suddenly he amazed me by accusing me of betraying him to Muller during that last raid. I denied it, of course. I don't think he believed me, then he went away.'

'It sounds as if Bill believed what Amelia told him,' Gould said. 'And when did you last see Felix Muller, Mr Gash?'

'He came here a month ago,' Gash said, with a shudder. 'I'd always thought he must be dead. But he stood there alive and well – an old man, of course, like me, but just as frightening and evil as he always was. He threatened to kill me, and I know he would have done it. He forced me to give him Bill Cottrell's address, then he left.'

'And, as we both know, that led directly to Bill Cottrell's death,' Gould said. 'You could have told the police about Muller's visit and they could have protected Bill. How can you live with yourself knowing that you allowed an old friend and fellow-soldier to be tortured and killed like that?'

Gash was about to speak, but he merely stood there ashamed. Gould sighed. 'Your treachery during the war is probably too long ago to be dealt with by the courts. But allowing Bill Cottrell to be killed and tortured this year could lead to several different charges. I will have to think about what to do with them.'

'I'm sorry about what happened to Bill Cottrell, but no one thinks worse of me than I do,' Gash said, all his bravado disappearing.

'Let's move on,' Gould said. 'Can you tell us why you visited Corsica this year, Mr Gash?'

'As you can imagine, I was ashamed of what I had let happen to Bill Cottrell, when I betrayed him to Muller,' Gash said, sitting down. 'I realised how much damage Felix Muller had done to my life – forcing me to become a traitor to my country during the war and to betray my old friend recently. I realised how much I still hated him, even if we were both old men now. When Muller was here, he talked about looking for some treasure he thought was buried in Bastia. I think I had some crazy idea of stopping him in some way – perhaps I wanted to kill him, I don't know. For whatever reason, I flew to Corsica, then wandered around Bastia for a couple of days. Then one day, I suddenly saw Muller's body in the water in the harbour. It could have been some sort of accident. If, as you say, he had been murdered, then I don't know who killed him, but it wasn't me.'

Fox took out his notebook and spoke for the first time. 'So, you are saying that you returned to Corsica after fifty years, with some vague plan to murder Muller, a man you had good reason to hate. You walk around Bastia then, by chance, you find that he had in fact just been killed. You say it was coincidental, but it all sounds very suspicious to me. And how soon after Muller was murdered did you leave Corsica, Mr Gash?'

'I left the next day. I didn't want to hang around,' Gash said. 'Someone had killed Muller. That was enough for me. I tried to forget about him and continue my life back here.'

'And have you returned to Corsica since then?' Gould asked.

'No.'

'A young woman named Zoe Vogel was murdered a week ago. You might not know her name, but does this picture mean anything to you?' Gould passed Gash a photo of Zoe.

'My God,' Gash said. 'That was the young woman who overheard Amelia and me arguing in the café in Bastia harbour. She threatened to tell the police what we had said. I gave her some money to keep her quiet, but she was alive when I left her. I wasn't in Corsica a week ago, anyway, so I couldn't have murdered her.'

'We believe that whoever killed Muller found some of these missing diamonds and is trying to sell them on the London market. Do you know anything about that?'

'No,' Gash replied, looking genuinely baffled. 'I don't know anything about any diamonds.'

Gould stood up and put his notebook away. 'Mr Gash, if there was any justice, you would be tried for your treachery during the war, and for conspiracy to fail to prevent the murder of your former officer, Bill Cottrell, earlier this year. As it is, it will be difficult to charge you with either of those matters. Now, I am investigating more recent events. You say you didn't kill Muller even though you were in Bastia harbour near the time he died. You had motive, means and opportunity, and I could make a convincing case for you being the murderer of Felix Muller.'

Gash looked around frightened, as if looking for someone else to blame. 'Amelia was there as well,' he said, pointing. 'We spoke afterwards. She could have killed Muller. She had as much motive as me.'

Amelia suddenly walked up to Gash and slapped his face twice. 'That is for betraying Bill all those years ago, and for trying to blame me now for Felix's murder. You snivelling coward. How dare you accuse me?'

Gould walked forward, grabbed Amelia's arms and pulled her away. 'Stop that, Madame Luri. I'm prepared to overlook this attack as you were provoked, but I want no more of this. Go out to the car.'

Gould stayed with Gash while Fox led a sobbing Amelia outside to wait in the police car.

'As I say, Mr Gash, I could make a strong case for arresting you for murdering Felix Muller in Bastia,' Gould said, keeping his eyes fixed on the terrified old man. 'You are also a suspect in the murder of Zoe Vogel, who you admit giving money to on the day of Muller's murder. You say you weren't in Corsica at the time of Zoe's murder, and we will have to investigate that. But I have several other lines of enquiry before I make an arrest. I will leave you now, Mr Gash, but don't go far away. I'm hoping I can wrap this case up in the next few days, so you won't have long to wait before knowing if you will be charged.'

'I will wait your call, but I tell you I didn't kill Muller. I wanted to, but I wouldn't have been brave enough.' Gash sat back in his chair, a defeated man. 'To be honest, I know I was a coward back in 1943 when I betrayed Bill Cottrell to Muller. And I was still a coward when I didn't have the guts to kill Muller this year.' He looked at Gould with a self-pitying expression. 'Think the worst of me, Chief Inspector, it's no worse than what I have called myself all these years. For better or worse, though, I am not a murderer. I enjoyed imagining killing Muller, but I wouldn't have the guts to do it for real.'

Gould looked at Gash. 'This interview has been very useful, Mr Gash. If you are innocent, you have nothing to worry about, apart from your own conscience. If you are guilty, I will be back quicker than you can ever imagine,' Gould said, standing up to leave. Gash stayed seated in his chair and did not show his visitor out.

When he was outside Gash's house, Gould went over to the unmarked car that he had arranged to follow him there. Detective Sergeant Fox wound down the window to talk to his superior officer.

'Foxy, I want you to stay here and follow Gash wherever he goes,' Gould said. 'He says he is too much of a coward to kill anyone, but I'm still suspicious. Follow him for the next couple of days.'

'Sure thing, gov,' Fox said. After Gould had left, taking Amelia back with him to her hotel, Fox waited for Gash to leave the house. Within an hour, Fox saw the front door open, and watched Gash climb into his car – an upmarket BMW. Fox followed Gash as he drove to the outskirts of London and then into the City. In Hatton Garden, Gash parked in an underground car park, took a key from his pocket, and entered a nondescript office building. Once Gash was inside, Fox made a note of the company's name and radioed Gould.

'You'll never believe this, gov,' Fox said, his voice rising in excitement. 'Gash entered the offices of a diamond trader called "Gash and Son". It looks as if he owns the company.'

Fox heard Gould cheer down the phone. 'So, Mr Gash knows a whole lot about diamonds, after all. He never told us that, did he? Keep following him, Foxy. I want to know where he goes.'

CHAPTER 49

Two days later, Philippa phoned Gould from Bastia. 'Karl and I have been keeping an eye on Link's yacht. He has gone out for a couple of days sailing, but I haven't found anything useful so far.'

'In that case, you'd better come home, Philippa. I'm pretty sure we will find the killer here with the preparation I have done so far.'

'Should I suggest Karl comes to London as well?'

'Yes, definitely, I want him here,' Gould said, almost shouting, then continued more normally. 'That is, please ask him to come. He will enjoy being in at the final act.'

'I'll ask him to come, gov. What about Link and Davies?'

'I'd like them here in London as well, where I can deal with them without having to go through the local police. Tell Davies I'm planning a raid to wrap up this case here in the City next week. If I know anything, he will rush to London to see what's happening and probably bring his friend, Mr Link, with him.'

* * * *

Later that day, Philippa made a courtesy visit to Dupree. 'Thank you for all your help, Andre,' she said, as they shook hands. 'Is Sergeant Clement here? I haven't seen him lately.'

'No, he is on leave for a couple of weeks. He is visiting London for a holiday, by coincidence,' Dupree said, repeating the lie he had concocted with Gould.

'Why is he in London?' Philippa asked.

'I think he may have friends there,' Dupree replied. 'Why? Did you need to see him?'

'No, just thank him for me,' Philippa said, in a light-hearted tone. Inwardly, Philippa had some concerns. The one thing certain about Muller's killer was that he had been in London, selling diamonds. Why would Clement be visiting London? It was unusual for Corsicans to travel to the cold of England for a holiday, and Clement had never mentioned friends or relatives in London. Philippa resolved to let Gould know about this. She would keep an eye open for Clement in any further investigation in London.

* * * *

The next day Gould, Philippa and Karl sat round a conference table at Snow Hill police station.

'Welcome back, Philippa and welcome to London, Karl.' Karl acknowledged with a polite nod. 'We have to follow up this inquiry at the London end,' Gould said. 'The Corsican police are following up on Muller and whoever killed him – that is out of our hands. Someone in London is selling a large number of diamonds. That person must be involved in the murder of Muller and your grandfather, Philippa, but how can we corner him?'

Karl spoke up. 'We can interview the dealers after the event and hope they recognise the seller. But whoever it is seems an expert in disguise and after he left, it may be too late to collar him.'

'I suggest we set up our own dummy dealership and hope the killer turns up there,' Philippa said. 'That seems promising. It will take some doing, though. It would mean making up a whole fictitious company. It would take some time to build up a reputation in the market.'

'Not necessarily,' Gould said. 'There are loads of freelance traders in the market. I'm proposing we could set up as a new solo trader and advertise for business.'

Karl smiled. 'That would be great. I suggest we advertise ourselves as soon as we can.'

Gould nodded. 'I think that is the way forward. We'll borrow a room from an existing trader and try to trap the killer as soon as he tries to sell the diamonds.'

CHAPTER 50

The next day, as Philippa had coffee with Karl in Snow Hill police station, she tried hard to make sense of her feelings for him. Although Karl was an Interpol operative, and she had vowed to avoid going out with other police officers, she told herself she enjoyed his company. She wondered if things could get serious between them. She had not had a serious boyfriend for a couple of years. A few years previously, she had a relationship for a while with David Gould, but it had ended when he had cut too many corners to arrest a major criminal. A later relationship with a civilian who had been involved in the same case petered out after a while.

At the end of the working day, Karl turned to Philippa. 'So, what is there to do in London on a weekday night?' Karl asked. 'I don't fancy an evening in a hotel room on my own.'

'Well, there's a good Greek restaurant near my flat in Greenwich,' Philippa said. 'There is a fast rail service back to your hotel afterwards.'

'That will be great, but it's my treat,' Karl said.

'We'll go there now,' Philippa said. 'But let's each pay our own way. In English, we call it going Dutch.'

'A Dutchman going Dutch,' Karl said, with a smile. 'I like it.'

* * * *

'It looks like the case is coming to an end, Karl. Gash is looking like the main suspect at the moment. We'll have to confirm he was in Corsica when Zoe was killed, and that should wrap up the case,' Philippa said, after they had ordered their meals. 'So, what are your plans for what to do after this case? I guess you'll be going back to Corsica, or will it be home to Amsterdam?'

'Oh, I'm just a foot soldier,' Karl replied, with a half-smile. 'I go where I am told. I try not to look too far ahead. You say Gash is guilty, but I think Dupree is a stooge of the Mafia and is involved somehow. I hope we can put him behind bars soon. I'm sure he's crooked. It makes me sick he can be a policeman but, all the while taking orders from the Mafia. I suppose as police officers, we see the worst of humanity, but that shocks even me.'

'Did I tell you Sergeant Clement is in London? He's supposed to be on holiday here, but, from what you say about the Corsican police, I wonder if he is really working for the Mafia in some way.'

'That's very interesting. We must keep an eye out for Clement. You may be right that he is working for Santoni.'

'Here we are, talking shop, on an evening out,' Philippa said, trying to lighten the mood. 'Let's talk about London. What do you think of it here?'

'Oh, I like the views, especially from where I'm sitting,' Karl said, looking at Philippa's face.

Philippa smiled demurely. 'I've enjoyed working with you, Karl,' she said. 'We must keep in touch when this is all over.'

Karl took her hands. 'Why don't you show me your flat?' he asked. 'I've had enough of hotel rooms.'

After the meal, Karl walked Philippa home. He kissed her goodnight, and she invited him in. She brought him a glass of wine and they started to chat. Before they had finished the glass, Karl held Philippa in his arms and kissed her with pent-up passion.

After a while, Philippa managed to free herself. 'We shouldn't be doing this, you know, Karl,' she said.

'Yes, it's probably against all sorts of police regulations,' Karl said, laughing as he started to remove Philippa's dress. She allowed Karl to lead her into her bedroom. The two of them spent the night together. When they woke up side by side in the morning, Philippa wondered what would happen to them in the future. All she knew was that she wanted to spend a long time with Karl, as a happy and well-matched couple.

CHAPTER 51

The next day, Gould and Fox knocked on the door of Gash and Son in Hatton Garden. After explaining their business to the receptionist, they were asked to await Tony Gash's arrival. While they were waiting, Fox looked out of the window at the fine views from Gash's office. The open area close to Saint Paul's cathedral lay below.

'You have a fine view of Paternoster Square from up here,' he said. 'It's a great open area down there.'

'Yes, not long ago, these buildings seemed the future, but now they're all out of fashion,' the receptionist started, but stopped when Gash entered with a face like thunder.

'What do you want now? I've told you everything I know,' Gash asked. 'You'd better come in if you want to see me.'

'Thank you for seeing us at such short notice, Mr Gash,' Gould said, once the door was closed. 'You never told us you were a diamond trader.'

'I don't believe you ever asked.'

'When we spoke, you said you didn't know anything about diamonds. Now we find you've spent your life in the business. That sounds very suspicious to me.'

'I said I didn't know anything about any stolen diamonds in Corsica, which I don't. I run a respectable business dealing in legitimate diamonds. I don't deal in stolen goods.'

'I understand, but I thought you might have offered to lend us your expertise in catching the murderer of Muller and Bill Cottrell,' Gould said.

'If I can help the police, I would be happy to.'

'Keep an eye out for anyone selling suspiciously large

210

amounts of diamonds, won't you, Mr Gash?' Gash nodded. 'We are mounting an operation near here to catch someone who should be able to provide useful information to catch the killer of Muller and Zoe Vogel.'

'I wish you luck, but I don't see how I can help,' Gash said.

'Just let us know if you hear of any stolen diamonds, won't you, Mr Gash?' Gould said in a firm tone.

Gash did not reply as the two police officers left his office.

CHAPTER 52

Two days later, in Snow Hill police station, Gould called Philippa and Karl into his office. 'It's looking like good news. We've recorded someone on video, trying to sell diamonds to our dummy dealer. It looks like one of the suspected crew members. He was trying to sell large amounts. No legitimate person could come by that much unless he was a trader. Foxy's shown his picture to the dealers around Hatton Garden, and no one recognises him, so he's looking suspicious.

'Our staff have asked him to come back on Tuesday and he's expecting us to buy the diamonds then. I suggest the three of us meet up with him instead and make an arrest. How does that sound?'

'I agree,' Karl said. 'Now we have him here, we must arrest him while we can. We can't afford to let him escape back to Corsica. I've said before we can't trust Dupree and some of the Corsican police. We must keep a special eye open for Sergeant Clement.'

'Neither of us believe Clement's story that he is in London on holiday,' Philippa told Gould.

'Can we look at the case against Clement,' Karl said. 'He could be involved. What do we know about this Walter, Philippa?'

'He is in his late thirties and has fair hair.'

'Does that remind you of anyone?' Karl asked.

'You're saying that Clement could be Walter?' Philippa asked.

'Think about it. How many Corsicans with fair hair did you see while you were over there, David?'

'Not many, now I think about it,' Gould admitted.

'So, I think Clement must be a suspect,' Karl said. 'He's in

London now – supposedly on holiday. I think Clement might be a bent copper.'

'Yes, you've made a good case. We'll keep an eye out for him. Now, whoever he is, I'm guessing the perpetrator's probably armed, and won't come without a fight,' Gould said. 'We need to get armed ready for the arrest. Come down to the gun marshal's office.'

Gould led Philippa and Karl down to the basement where they were all issued with service revolvers. The gun marshal made sure that each officer had their own set of bullets.

'This should conclude the investigation and we should be able to make an arrest,' Gould told Philippa and Karl as they returned to their desks. Once Gould was back into his own office, he made sure the door was closed before he made a phone call to the police in Corsica. 'Anton,' he called once Dupree had answered. 'We are close to making an arrest. I'd like you here to witness it.'

'Very well,' Dupree said, after a pause. 'I'll catch tonight's flight.'

'Sergeant Clement is already here in London, of course.'

'He says it's expensive and cold there, but I didn't have much sympathy,' Dupree added with a chuckle.

Soon after hanging up on the call to Dupree, Gould phoned the Ministry of Defence and asked to be put through to Christopher Davies. 'It's Colonel Davies here,' the public-school accent came over the phone. 'Chris, that is.'

'How do you do, Colonel,' Gould said, without warmth. 'I've read Philippa's report on your meeting with Edwin Link. I was disappointed you met a suspect without our knowledge. You told us you were returning to London after that first meeting with Dupree.'

'Yes, I'm sorry about that, but I do have useful information that will help you in your inquiry.' Davies waited for a response, but Gould did not reply. 'I've been wondering how Muller found out where Bill Cottrell was living.'

'We know about that,' Gould said. 'We know Muller threatened Tony Gash and he revealed the information.'

'Yes, but how did he track Gash down? Suppose you were Muller or Muller's accomplice, what would you do first if you wanted to track down Cottrell?'

'I suppose I would try the army to see if they knew where Bill Cottrell was,' Gould said, after a moment's thought. 'I assume army records would be bound to have that information as they paid his pension every month. But they wouldn't give his address out. They'd keep it in confidence.'

'That's exactly what army records said, when someone phoned up a week before Bill Cottrell was killed. But my colleagues kept a note of who phoned to request it.'

'Who was it? Did Muller give his name?'

'No. It wasn't Muller,' Davies said, his voice rising in excitement. 'It was someone completely different ...'

Gould sat open-mouthed as Davies gave the name of the person who had phoned to request Cottrell's details. 'Thank you very much, Chris ... That's confirmed what I suspected. We should be making an arrest on Tuesday. You might like to join us to see the end of this case.'

* * * *

'We need to have a final meeting,' Gould said on Tuesday morning. Karl, Philippa and Fox sat at the table with Gould. 'There's no doubt that the Mafia are behind Muller's murder and the sale of diamonds. The man selling them must be some sort of Mafia stooge. If we can arrest him, he will be able to direct us to the real murderer. I've asked Anton Dupree to come to London. If he is really working with the Mafia, he should be worried. He's on our turf now and if he is guilty, we can arrest him. What do you think, Karl?'

'I've always said I am suspicious of Dupree,' Karl replied. 'He is too close to Santoni and the rest of the Mafia. If the man we arrest tomorrow is a small-scale criminal, he may want to shop Santoni and Dupree to save his own neck. That should provide great evidence against both of them.'

'I've just received more information that seems to point to Dupree being guilty.'

'What was that?' Philippa asked.

'I'd rather keep that to myself for the moment,' Gould said. 'Come on, this is going to be exciting,' he added. 'Do you have the guns we've been issued?'

'Yes, all ready,' both Karl and Philippa said in unison.

'We're getting to be like a couple, finishing each other's sentences,' Karl said.

'I think we are,' Philippa said thoughtfully, as she smiled at Karl. Gould looked at them both and shook his head.

* * * *

The site of the sale was to be close to Paternoster Square and Karl and Philippa looked around. Paternoster Square lay close to St Paul's Cathedral in the City of London. It had been built after the war, following the bombing that had erased the previous Victorian buildings. It was composed of an open square surrounded by low-level sixties office buildings. When it was built it had won several architectural awards, but by the late nineties it was vaguely depressing. Philippa told herself it posed an interesting contrast – Sir Christopher Wren's magnificent cathedral nearby was still widely admired, while the ephemera of the sixties architecture was despised.

'Do you think anyone ever really admired these buildings?' Philippa asked, vaguely.

'I guess so,' Karl replied in a dubious tone. 'I'd like to look around to become familiar with this area. We don't want the Mafia doing some sort of shoot-out to protect their man.'

As Karl walked around the area of Paternoster Square, he did not know that he was being followed. Clement made a note of Karl's movements and reported them to the man who gave him orders.

CHAPTER 53

The following morning, Paulu checked his appearance in the mirror of his budget hotel room. He had never been to the City of London before, and he wanted to be sure he was smart enough to blend into his surroundings. He felt he needed a second opinion.

'Maman,' he called out.

Amelia walked in from the next room. 'Yes, Cheri?'

'How do I look?'

'You look fine,' Amelia replied, adjusting her son's tie. 'Have you made a note of your lines?'

'Yes, Maman, but I'm frightened,' Paulu said, before continuing after a pause. 'It may not be the right time to ask, but I may be killed today so there may not be another chance. There's one thing I want to know. Did you ever love my father?'

Amelia looked at Paulu sadly. 'I slept with Felix Muller to save my life. People were starving in those days,' she said. 'I always hated him. You know, I was never a traitor. I helped the Resistance as much as I could. I was still seeing my husband at the time, and I honestly don't know who your father was, Paulu.'

'I told Muller I was his son. He thought I looked like him.'

'You may have been Felix's son. I hope not though.'

'Do you know who killed Muller?' Paulu asked. 'I wouldn't blame you if you had killed him, after what he put you through.'

'No, I didn't kill Felix,' Amelia said, 'but I'd like to shake his killer's hand, whoever he was. Most Corsicans think whoever killed Felix was a hero – and so do I.'

'What would you think of me if I killed Muller?'

'You'll always be my son, and I'll always be proud of you. I can't believe you killed him – did you?'

'Of course not.'

'I couldn't bear you to go to prison, Paulu. You wouldn't last five minutes there. It's a strange thing to say about my own son, but I'd rather kill you than let that happen.'

Paulu stood up, ready to leave. 'Never mind about that. Do you think my life is in danger today, Maman?'

'I don't know. We have to rely on Mr Gould to protect us,' Amelia said. 'One thing is for sure, though.'

'What's that?'

'We're safer here than in Corsica.'

'It won't be so bad if we get this reward money that Gould promised. We could live comfortably anywhere in France. Let's go now,' Paulu said, then stopped dead as he heard a knock on the hotel door. 'Who can that be?' he asked before peering through the spy hole in the door. 'It's Sergeant Clement. What's he doing here? Why isn't he in Bastia?'

'I don't know, but let him in,' Amelia said.

Paulu opened the door carefully. 'Sergeant Clement, isn't it? We weren't expecting you.'

'Inspector Gould asked me to pick you up and take you to the rendezvous,' Clement said. 'I'm involved in the case, and he thought you might welcome a familiar face from Corsica,' he added with a slight smile.

'He never mentioned it, but I guess it's all right,' Amelia said. 'Come along, Paulu.'

Clement ushered Amelia and Paulu down to a black car and drove them away. As he was driven along, Paulu read through his prepared lines again, and shook with fear as he looked out at the city streets, so different from his home in Corsica. He did not realise that the man they feared from their Corsican past was following in a limousine. Santoni had recognised Paulu and Amelia immediately. He knew they thought they were safe from him in London, but nothing was further from the truth. He recognised Sergeant Clement as well but took less notice of him.

Santoni often told his henchmen that he did not appreciate being made to look a fool. He knew that his career was based on building up a climate of fear around his Corsican base, and if the word got around that people were getting away with rival criminal activities, his comfortable lifestyle would be in jeopardy. For this reason, he told himself that killing Paulu was his best option.

Santoni had occasionally visited London as part of his criminal career and had built up a network of English gangsters that he knew he could rely on, in exchange for a generous sum of money. One of them had arranged for this car and driver. Santoni knew that passengers on flights to London were searched by British Customs and a firearm would be unlikely to be successfully smuggled through. For this reason, Santoni had entered the United Kingdom feeling naked as he was in the unusual position for him of not having a firearm on his person. He was grateful his British criminal colleagues had arranged to lend him the rifle that was now resting by his feet.

He told his driver to carry on following Paulu and Amelia. When they arrived at Hatton Garden, Santoni looked for a suitable vantage point from where he could keep an eye on developments.

* * * *

Tony Gash looked out of his office window down to Paternoster Square below. He felt proud of how he had built up the small-scale jewellers he had inherited from his father to the profitable company in the City of London he ran now. He had been shaken by his visit from Gould and Amelia a couple of days before. He accepted Gould's criticisms of the way he gave away Bill Cottrell's address when Muller had visited him.

Gash often thought back to his chat with Bill when they were still young men, back in 1945. Gash remembered that, for some reason that he had never understood at the time, Bill had asked about Hatton Garden. From what he knew now, Gash assumed that Bill had been trying to find a market for some diamonds he had illegally acquired in Corsica.

Gash felt it was ironic that he worked in Hatton Garden now. He was ashamed that Bill had found out about his treachery during the war, which had ended their friendship. He wondered if there was some way he could make amends to his late army colleague. He walked over to his safe and pulled out a bag of diamonds. He never tired of running these precious stones through his fingers.

Gould had told Gash that someone, probably Muller's murderer, was selling diamonds in London. He wondered if there was some way he could pretend to help the police investigation, as he returned to his desk and made a phone call.

* * * *

At a café close to Paternoster Square, Christopher Davies took two cups of coffee to the table he was sharing with Edwin Link. The coffee was instant, and the crockery was chipped. Link glared at Davies. 'Why are you in full uniform, Colonel?'

'I'm proud of my uniform – why shouldn't I wear it?' Davies replied, feeling his service revolver close to his hand.

Link grunted. 'I hope this trip to London will be worth my while, Colonel,' he said. 'This isn't the level of establishment that I usually frequent.'

'Oh, yes. I'm sure you will find your visit here interesting,' Davies replied. 'Gould told me he is hoping to make an arrest on this case near here soon. I have my radio tied up to the police frequencies so we can check on developments in the case.'

Link looked coldly at Davies. 'Do you really know what's going on, Colonel?'

'I will go and find out the latest developments, Mr Link,' Davies said, as he prepared to leave the café.

'Very well,' Link said, pushing his unfinished cup of instant coffee to one side. 'I expect you to keep me informed.'

CHAPTER 54

Paulu looked up at the City of London office block in Paternoster Square and felt the small pieces of glass in his pocket. He had left his mother drinking a coffee in a nearby café with Sergeant Clement. Now that he was on his own, he was feeling petrified, as he inwardly ran through the forms of words he had been given to say.

For a moment, Paulu wanted to back down from the charade that Gould had arranged. He did not feel at home in these cold London streets and wished he could be back in the warmth of Corsica. After a moment's hesitation, he reflected he had been given little or no choice other than to cooperate with the City of London police. Gould had told him that this was the only way he could prove he did not kill Muller or Zoe. Trying to calm his nerves, he approached the receptionist, in reality a member of Gould's team.

'Can I help you, sir?' the undercover DS Fox asked.

'Yes, I would like to sell some diamonds. How much will you give me for them?' Paulu asked, using the lines he had been coached by Gould.

'Certainly, sir,' Fox replied, pulling a spy glass from his pocket to examine the merchandise.

In the tiny office next to the reception, Karl turned to Philippa. 'That looks like the mystery man who's selling the diamonds from Corsica,' he whispered.

'Yes, that must be him,' Philippa said. 'We'll make a move on my signal.'

While Karl and Philippa watched through the two-way mirror, Fox continued to talk to Paulu. 'These are fine stones, sir,' Fox said. 'May I ask how you came by these?'

'Oh, I inherited them from my mother. They have been in my family for many years …' Paulu began his prepared speech. Before he could finish his sentence, Karl and Philippa rushed in. Paulu fell back terrified as the two police officers pinned his arms back and put handcuffs on his wrists. Gould followed them in and watched developments.

'Don't resist,' Philippa said. 'Paulu Luri, you are under arrest for selling stolen diamonds, and possibly several murders. You are not obliged to say anything, but anything you do say may be used in evidence against you.'

'But I'm innocent,' Paulu said. 'I haven't done anything.'

'We'll see about that,' Philippa replied, through gritted teeth.

'Karl, take our suspect to the car,' Gould said. 'We'll interrogate him at the station. Stay with me, Philippa.'

Karl led Paulu to the car while the City of London detectives conferred at the site of the interrupted pretend transaction. Only Gould and Fox knew that the supposed diamonds were fake.

'Well done, Foxy,' Gould said, shaking Fox's hand. 'You were very convincing.' Just then they heard a gunshot ring out. Rushing outside, Philippa saw Karl standing above Paulu, who was lying on the ground, his shirt stained with red.

'My God, Karl, what happened?' Philippa asked.

'I heard a rifle shot from one of the buildings,' Karl replied, pointing at a nearby skyscraper. 'His accomplices must have realised he was under arrest and were trying to rescue him,' Karl said. 'I couldn't let him get away, and I fired back. In the melee, I'm afraid the suspect was hit.'

Gould knelt down to the body and checked his pulse. 'My God, he's dead,' he said. 'He could have had valuable information. Tell us again exactly what happened.'

'It must have been another one of the thieves probably trying to rescue this man. Or he might have got greedy and his colleagues wanted to eliminate him,' Karl said, looking panicked.

'I did fire a shot. I aimed at the top of that skyscraper where the shots came from. I can't tell if I hit any of the gang.'

'Wasn't there any other way to stop him escaping?' Philippa asked. 'He was our prime witness. Now he's dead and we have no other leads. The top men will never face justice. Let's see if we can capture any of the gang. Can you be sure where the shots came from?'

'I'm sure it was that building over there,' Karl said, pointing to a nearby office block.

'Would you recognise the person who shot our suspect, Karl?' Gould asked, coldly. 'It would be useful to have a description.'

'It was a tall fair man dressed in black. I can't be sure, but he did look very like Clement,' Karl said. 'I told you I was suspicious about the Corsican police. Put out an all-points bulletin for Clement. I'm sure we could find him very soon with all your police resources on the case.'

'It seems to be quiet now,' Philippa said. 'Was it necessary for you to shoot back?'

'I may have been hasty to shoot, but you wouldn't give evidence against me, would you, Philippa?' Karl asked, with what he hoped was a winning smile.

'I would have to if there is an investigation, Karl. That's my job,' Philippa said.

'It won't be very hard to find Sergeant Clement,' Gould said. 'He is behind me now. Come forward, Sergeant. Karl thinks you shot the suspect.'

'No, I've been keeping an eye on Karl as you said, Chief Inspector. It was him who shot the suspect – for no legal reason.'

'Tell us the truth, Karl,' Philippa said. 'If you made a mistake, I'm sure we can work this out.'

Karl swivelled round to point his gun at Philippa. His demeanour had changed from his cultured image to that of a frightened criminal. 'I'm afraid I can't allow that to happen. Lovely as you are, if you try to stop me, I will have to kill you.' Karl grabbed Philippa from behind.

'My God, Karl. What are you doing?' Philippa screamed.

Gould came up behind Karl. 'Put that gun down, Karl. It's all over. You can't escape now.'

Karl responded by grabbing Philippa even tighter. 'I will kill you as well if I have to, David.'

Gould stretched out his hand. 'Give me that gun, Karl. You have killed too many people already.'

'Four to be precise,' Karl said, his voice rising with pride. 'I am happy to make it six if you and Philippa try to stop me.'

Gould stared without emotion at Karl. 'Just hand over the gun, Karl,' he said. 'You can't get away. I've known for a while that you're the guilty man – the one who helped Muller kill Bill Cottrell and then killed Muller and Zoe. You took the fake name of Walter, and it's you who's been trying to sell Rommel's diamonds you stole from Muller around London.'

'Very well, you can die as well, if you insist,' Karl said. 'I am sorry about this, David. I have nothing against you, but I'm not going to prison,' he added, raising the gun to Gould's chest. 'Say your prayers now, David,' he added, pulling the trigger. Philippa screamed, 'No, Karl don't do it!' as Karl fired at Gould with what he hoped was a fatal shot. For a moment, he was satisfied with his accuracy, but then stood there stunned when Gould remained standing.

'You're wasting your time, Karl. I've been suspicious of you for a long time. You used the name Walter as a disguise. You tortured and killed Bill Cottrell, then later killed Muller. You were the corrupt policeman in Corsica – not Dupree or Clement. Then you killed Zoe. You must have realised she recognised you as the killer, when you interrogated her in Berlin. She was lying about Link being the killer – she was probably hoping to blackmail you. Beneath your charm, you're nothing more than a heartless murderer,' Gould gave a slight chuckle. 'That's why I made sure your gun was filled with blank bullets. You can't kill me or Philippa, and you haven't killed this man. Stand up now, Paulu.'

Paulu, who had appeared to be dead, started to move. 'Did I do good, Mr Gould?' he asked, when he was standing.

Karl looked horrified. 'What the hell's going on? I just killed this man.'

'You thought you did,' Gould said. He turned to Paulu. 'Well done, Paulu. You fell down dead when the blank sounded, just as I told you. If you can give evidence against the real murderer, I'm sure the Corsican police will be lenient with you. Now, Paulu Luri, do you recognise this man?' he asked, pointing at Karl.

Paulu stared at Karl. 'He had different coloured hair. I guess he was wearing a wig when he was on the yacht, but yes, that person is the man I know as Walter.'

'Liar!' Karl screamed. 'This man is nothing more than a crook. He seems to have even stolen diamonds from me.'

'No, that was my little trick,' Gould said. 'Paulu made a confession to being on the yacht, but he didn't have any diamonds. Those were cut glass he was pretending to sell. He didn't know much about your plot, but he could recognise the man who was on his crew. That was you. I reckoned if you thought he had double crossed you, you would incriminate yourself in some way. And you did, didn't you? As he says, you were Walter, the third man on the yacht. I thought you would try to kill Paulu, so he couldn't identify you. I saw how shocked you were when you realised the bullets were blank.'

'How did you know?' Karl asked, his face filled with hate, as Fox put handcuffs on him. All Karl's superficial charm had drained away from him by this stage, and he seemed like a weak man consumed by evil. Suddenly, Gould realised what Mr Samuelson had meant, when he said the person selling the diamonds, who Gould now knew was Karl, seemed to be a Nazi from an earlier time.

'You were the prime suspect to me, but I never told Philippa,' Gould said. 'I knew that if I set up Paulu as having the diamonds, you would try to kill him. Those blank bullets I arranged to be loaded into your gun made a lot of noise but didn't do any damage. Paulu pretended to play dead, as I told him to.

'The final proof was that the army records office told us they had received a request from you for Bill Cottrell's address. The only reason for you to want that information before Bill was killed was that you were Muller's accomplice. You shouldn't have given your real name. That was a bad mistake.'

'Why not?' Karl said, shrugging his shoulders. 'I was a cop hunting Rommel's gold. I thought an official request might be more effective.'

'One thing I would like to know,' Gould asked. 'Were you always going to kill Muller, or did you have an argument?'

'Oh, yes, I was always going to kill Muller. He was an evil old man who deserved to die,' Karl said. 'Killing that old fool Cottrell was collateral to allow me to get my hands on those diamonds. Zoe was just a tart who knew too much. She had to be killed.'

Philippa stood up close to Karl. 'How could you treat me in that way, Karl? You killed my grandfather, and then you led me on. You're supposed to uphold the law – not cooperate with men like Muller. What sort of man are you anyway?'

Karl smiled wryly. 'I used to be an honest policeman in Interpol in Amsterdam. I had a small salary and knew I had to wait forty years for a pension. I didn't want that life. Then I was posted to Corsica. While I was researching Rommel's diamonds, I found out that Muller was still alive. I realised being Muller's accomplice was likely to be more profitable than trying to arrest him. I did enjoy our time together, Philippa, but money is much more important to me than love.'

'You and Muller seem to be of a similar character,' Gould said. 'And now you're going to end up in prison – where Muller should have been, until you killed him. For the record, how did you meet Muller?'

'From immigration records, I'd learnt he was arriving in Corsica. I met him, then offered myself as an associate and a crew member for his expedition to recover Rommel's treasure. Together Muller and I tortured that silly old man here in London. Once he told us what he knew, we killed him. I didn't feel guilty. He wouldn't have lived long, anyway.'

Philippa stood up and slapped Karl. 'That's for Grandad and that's for lying to me,' she said, slapping him again. Karl's whole body shook as red marks appeared on his cheek.

Gould stood up and opened the back door of the police car where Dupree had been waiting. 'We have your prisoner ready for you, Anton.' Turning to Karl, he said, 'Anton Dupree has a cell waiting for you in Corsica. I don't envy the life sentence you'll get. Once the other prisoners know you are an ex-policeman with bags of diamonds hidden away somewhere, I doubt if your life will be worth living.'

'What's he doing here?' Karl asked. 'I told you not to tell him about me.'

'Hello, Karl,' Dupree said. 'We meet at last. I gather you've been telling everyone I'm in the pay of the Mafia. Do you know how many years I've been fighting Santoni and people like him? Do you know how many death threats I've received from criminals in my career? Then you come along and blacken my name. I will enjoy putting you away for life.'

'You told me you would keep my identity a secret, Gould,' Karl shouted. 'You promised not to let this man know about me.'

'I've told Anton about you all along. You're not the only one who can lie, Karl,' Gould said. 'I knew Anton is a decent cop, and I trusted him – unlike you. We worked together well, didn't we, Anton?'

'Yes, I learnt all about you, Karl, as soon as David met you,' Dupree said. He followed Fox, who forcibly removed Karl down to the cells.

Once Karl had been taken away, Philippa, shaking with emotion, turned to Gould. 'To think I trusted Karl. What a fool I've been, I never dreamt he killed Grandad. I know I was wrong to slap Karl. It was unprofessional, but I couldn't stop myself. I shouldn't have let him chat me up during the enquiry, but I thought we were friends. I guess I am not as good a detective as I thought I was.'

'Philippa, you're a fine detective. I'm sorry I couldn't tell you the whole truth before now. You've just been deceived by an evil man, which can happen to anyone,' Gould said then winked at Philippa. 'Did you slap Karl, Philippa? I didn't notice. I must have been looking away.'

'Thank you, David, for keeping quiet on that,' Philippa said. 'Now, is there any way of keeping Grandad's name out of any court case? I'd like to keep his good name. He made a mistake when he was still young, but he didn't deserve to die in the way he did. In my nightmares, I can still imagine those thugs torturing him.'

'Don't worry,' Gould said. 'In my report, I'll say we have no evidence that Bill was anything other than an honest copper. I'll pretend we only have Karl's word that Bill stole those diamonds. Karl spent his whole life lying. Why should anyone believe him now? The coroner gave a verdict of suicide while his mind was disturbed on your father. Let's leave it like that. Saying he was murdered would only lead to questions about what he did during the war.

'We'll send Karl back to Corsica as I promised him. The case is stronger that he killed Muller than he killed Bill. Karl may receive some public sympathy for killing Muller, but I'll make sure Dupree charges him with Zoe's murder as well. The jury won't like the thought of a young girl being killed for money, and that will be sure to lead to a life sentence. If Karl was charged in this country, he would be sure to drag Bill's name down into the gutter. Charging him in Corsica means Bill can keep his good name in death …'

'Thanks again, David. That means a lot to me.' Philippa looked at a display of diamonds in the window of a nearby trading room.

'You know, the love of diamonds eventually killed Grandad. And if Karl hadn't learnt about Rommel's treasure, he might have remained an honest policeman. I've decided I'm never going to wear diamonds ever again.'

'You may be right. I've never seen their appeal. They are only crushed carbon after all. There was no reason for all this to happen.'

'Do you think Karl still has some of Rommel's diamonds stashed away?'

'Come on, Philippa,' Gould said. 'That's not our business anymore. We'll leave Anton Dupree to handle it now. I think the best thing is for us to move on to our next case. But there is something else we need to do.'

Gould turned to the police officers dressed as ambulance men who had arrived to take Paulu's body away. 'Please lie down on the stretcher, Mr Luri. We want anyone watching to think you are dead. Afterwards, you will be taken to a safe house. You will probably have to give evidence against Karl – the man you knew as Walter. You will be fully protected, of course. After that, you and your mother can live in either London or France, but I suggest you avoid returning to Corsica. I'll recommend you receive the reward from De Beers. It will be up to £50,000. That should help you and your mother to start a new life.'

'Thank you, Mr Gould,' Paulu said, shaking Gould's hand. Paulu obediently lay down on the stretcher while the pretend ambulance men pulled the sheet over him. As Gould had previously arranged, the top of Paulu's head remained visible, making him recognisable. Gould attended the stretcher with an appropriately solemn expression as it was laid into the back of the ambulance. Amelia, playing the role of a grief-stricken mother, clutched a handkerchief as she accompanied the stretcher into the ambulance.

* * * *

From a distance, Santoni saw the stretcher being taken into the waiting ambulance. He recognised Paulu from the top of his head and watched Paulu's apparently lifeless body being loaded on to the ambulance, accompanied by his weeping mother. Santoni shrugged as he put his binoculars down and started to dismantle the rifle he had borrowed for the occasion. Paulu appeared to be dead, without any intervention from Santoni. He did not know who killed him, but decided to make a quick exit before the City of London police asked awkward questions.

Paulu had originally appeared to Santoni to be a useful tool towards finding the gold and diamonds that the Nazis had left behind in Corsica. Now, he had apparently been killed by the police or by other criminals. Such a death was an occupational hazard in the crime business, and, to Santoni, Paulu was merely a potentially useful tool that had apparently been eliminated. Santoni reflected that this was, in many ways, the best of outcomes for him – he could boost his image by boasting that he had killed Paulu for straying out of line, without having the dangers of actually committing the murder. He had no doubt that people would believe that he had killed Paulu.

After a moment's thought, Santoni put the idea of retrieving Rommel's diamonds aside as he planned his next criminal adventure. It would not have occurred to Santoni to mourn Paulu's apparent death, but he did curse the end of his pursuit of the diamonds. In a few months' time, Santoni would see Paulu, very much alive, give evidence against Karl in a Corsican court. Santoni would be furious at the deception, but by then, Paulu and Amelia would be living under police protection in a remote part of the French countryside. They would be far away from Santoni's revenge.

* * * *

From a coffee bar on the other side of Paternoster Square, Edwin Link and Christopher Davies watched the ambulance taking the apparently lifeless Paulu away.

'What do you think, Edwin?' Davies asked. 'It looks as if the police have shot the person who was trying to sell the diamonds you've been looking for all these years. What are you going to do now?'

Link snorted. 'Carry on looking, of course. I still say there is more treasure hidden away in the sea near Corsica, if I can only find it. Goodbye, Colonel, I won't need your services anymore.'

Davies left, disappointed to have lost a way of generating an illicit income from his knowledge of the history of the Second World War. He looked behind him to see Link happily preparing for his next expedition around Corsica. It was obvious that Edwin Link was sure there was plenty more treasure in the seas around Corsica, if he could only find it. To him, the excitement of the race to find Rommel's diamonds was everything.

* * * *

Tony Gash put away the papers he was working on and prepared to leave his office. He had heard some commotion down in the square outside but thought no more of it. Gash decided he would stick to his regular trade in jewellery. He felt he had had too much excitement over the past year and walked down to the station to make his way home. He looked forward to another evening with his ex-army colleagues at the British Legion. He would regale his friends with his fictional tales of heroism in Corsica when he was a young man. Gash knew that he was a coward, and always had been, but saw no reason to broadcast this fact to his friends.

CHAPTER 55

A month later, Philippa Cottrell placed a bunch of roses on the gravestone that read 'William Cottrell 1919 to 1994'. She bowed her head in respect to her late grandfather. She remembered how the sight of him in his smart constable's uniform when she was a child had inspired her to join the police. He had been the last surviving member of her family, and, now he was dead, she supposed she must face the world alone.

Philippa reminded herself that her grandfather had been a brave soldier and police officer for most of his life. She realised his one moment of greed at the end of the war tarnished her memory of him. She did not know if she would ever think of him in the same way as she used to, before she knew about his theft of part of the treasure that Muller had forced him to transport in Corsica.

The greed for diamonds seemed to have been too much for both her grandfather and the man she might have grown to love. She knew that Karl was now in a Corsican jail in solitary confinement. This was to protect him from the other prisoners who felt he must still have a large amount of money stored away somewhere, if only they could frighten him into revealing it. She shuddered with shame when she recalled her night of passion with Karl. She tried not to visualise Muller and Karl torturing then killing her grandfather in his old age, but the more she tried not to dwell on it, the more painful the speculations that came into her thoughts.

'I thought I would find you here,' a voice said behind Philippa. She turned and saw David Gould looking kindly at her.

'Oh, hello, gov,' she said. 'I just wanted to leave some flowers for my grandfather. At least we've avenged his murder as much as we can. He was a good man really, you know. I'll never forgive Karl for what he did to Grandad. To think, I thought that awful man was a friend – even a lover.'

'You should remember Bill as the honest hard-working police officer he was for most of his life. Together, we did our best for his memory. We put Karl behind bars, where he belongs. He will be sure to suffer for the rest of his life. I wouldn't want to be in Karl's shoes now, fearing that the next knock on his cell door will be from the Mafia,' Gould said.

'What can we do about the money Grandad stole, David? It makes me sick to think that our family gained from Nazi gold.'

'It's too late to worry about that, Philippa,' Gould said.

'Thanks for everything, David,' Philippa said, as Gould held her to stop her from fainting with relief.

'I wanted to have a word, Philippa,' Gould said, after a few moments. 'I know it's good to mourn your grandfather, but I think it's time you moved on, don't you? I never met him, but I'm sure Bill would have wanted you to keep on being a good detective for the rest of your career. There are plenty of other crimes for us to solve. We've just had a call at the station. It's a tricky murder – the perfect case for you.'

Philippa looked from the grave to her boss. She told herself her grandfather was in many ways a casualty of war, even though his death took place fifty years after the fall of Nazi Germany. She knew it was undoubtedly time to put the awful events of the war behind her and move on with her City of London detective work into present-day crimes.

'Tell me about it, gov. It sounds an interesting case. Do you have any suspects yet?' Philippa asked. She followed Gould out of the graveyard, as she listened to the details of their next case.

9 781789 633429